THE STEAM ROOM DIARIES

CAMERON MILLER

THE STEAM ROOM DIARIES
CAMERON MILLER

Tumbleweed Books

Tumble through the pages of our books

HTTP://TUMBLEWEEDBOOKS.CA

An imprint of DAOwen Publications

The Steam Room Diaries / Cameron Miller

ISBN 978-1-928094-08-1
EISBN 978-1-928094-09-8

Cover art by Indigo Forest Designs

10 9 8 7 6 5 4 3 2 1

Acknowledgements

Gratitude is the active ingredient in healing, hope, and joy and considering the long course of this book, and who and what brought it to fruition, I am filled with thanksgiving.

Thanks to the followers of www.subversivepreacher.org, some of whom I know and many more who I have not met. You have expanded my vision and understanding of community and the connections made possible through writing.

Thanks to those who have helped me hone my story-telling and have been encouraging along the way, especially the people of Saint John's, Lafayette (IN); Saint Mathew's, Indianapolis (IN); Saint Stephen's, Columbus (O); Trinity, Buffalo (NY); and Saint Mark's, Newport (VT).

Thanks to Thom Rock and Sarah Baughman, eloquent writers and generous friends who inspired me to re-write the narrator, encouraged me always, and challenge me to be better.

Thanks to Tim Wadkins who gave me his office to write in and generously shared El Salvador with me.

Thanks to my former Canisius College students who sat through "Abraham's Children" together, and were an early audience for some of these stories.

Thanks to the summer *Steam Room Diaries* group at Trinity Church Buffalo who read and discussed early versions of some of these stories.

Many thanks to Lorene Potter for her early reviews; to both Sarah and Katy Miller who vigorously edited and encouraged me; and to Douglas Owen and Tumbleweed Books because they took this project on, then edited and helped make it better.

Finally, thanks to the strangers in steam rooms, saunas, on air planes, and at coffee shops that have told me amazing and intimate details of their lives for reasons I will never know. God bless you, my fellow travelers, and may you stumble upon the sacred at your feet.

A Note to the Reader

The Steam Room Diaries is a work of fiction.

If you think you recognize one of the characters in this novel, you do not. If you imagine that one of these characters is someone you know, or knew, in the steam room or from a fitness class where you work out, you don't.

The characters in this book are fictional and not based upon any known persons. Any similarity between actual and living persons with characters in this book is purely accidental. Any similarity between any actual places, other than the entire city of Buffalo, with any places described in this book, is unintentional.

The stories of sacredness, however, and encounters with the holy, are as real as the steam room itself. Remember, truth and fact are not the same things.

To James, Sarah, Abram, Anne, and Katy who have opened the envelope to the sacred in my life more times than I can count and probably more often than even I know. You saved my life and made it worth living ... and writing about.

Chapter One

Lumbini and the Steam Room

My mother calls me, "The Priest Who Couldn't Keep it in His Pants." She wasn't at all surprised, she tells her friends, because she knew her son wasn't up for the job. Then she laughs hysterically every time. I'm thinking about saving my therapy bills this year, putting them in a box, and wrapping it elegantly for Christmas. She won't laugh, I assure you.

That is not where I wanted to begin this story. I intended to begin with God, not my mother, though in the shadowed voices of my psyche they often get confused.

What comes with the collar does not disappear when the little white piece of plastic is stripped away; it is not something you are one day and not the next. There is something that lives in the lining of your stomach and shapes you from the inside out. You don't look any different, and most of the time you don't feel any different, although when it happens the map of your inscape changes. But there I go again, beginning the story with me when it wasn't what I meant to do.

Let me start over.

There is no such thing as a successful search for *the holy*, no hunting it down with specially trained bloodhounds of the soul chasing its scent over the landscape of time. Go looking for the holy and it won't be found. Don't look for it, stay open to it, and then, sometimes there it is.

Most people look for God in sanctuaries sculpted by human imagination, or in the magnificence of natural beauty. Clichés abound when it comes to God but most of them are bullshit. If it sounds too good to be true it probably isn't.

I know a brainiac who went off to M.I.T., an atheist, and says he found God studying mathematics. That's weird, but he would say encountering God in a steam room is bizarre. Even so, the steam room I frequent is a god spot. It's not so much an encounter with God as it is a prickling on the back of the neck whispering that some holy thing was here a moment ago and the air still tingles with mystic mojo.

A sacred place is anywhere God has left tracks in the mud of human experience; still there is no guarantee a seeker will catch up and peer into divine mystery by following them. Standing at the edge of Olduvai Gorge in Tanzania, where the crust of the earth is broken open and the inside of the loaf crumbles out, paleontologists stumbled upon the grandmother bones of our humanoid ancestry and the place is thick with sacredness.

The rolling battlefield of the Little Big Horn, its deep dry gulches and lonely cemetery hill, is crisscrossed and tangled with tracks running into and out of the sacred. At Lumbini, in the Himalayan foothills of Nepal, dangling toes in the placid pool of the peeling temple of Maya Devi, knowing that this was the very place where the Buddha was born, the tracks are so fresh and deep a pilgrim can almost put a hand into them.

In the little white steam room in the basement of the Robert L. Cohen Fitness Center in Buffalo, New York, you find fresh tracks of the holy left daily, just as you can see the newly pressed prints of deer and raccoon at the edge of a lake each morning.

The small rectangular steam room is floor to ceiling alabaster white tile, scrubbed in the merciless light of a single whining florescent fixture. It could, if you were on the edge of sanity, scream at you. There's nothing on its face to imply sacredness. It is, in fact, old and tired and in need of repair. But any place through which God routinely passes, a sacred space, requires neither beauty nor magnificence.

I visit the steam room almost every day, not so much to look for God as to reward myself for doing what I loathe. *Ten more minutes on this freakin' Stairmaster, then I can have an extra five minutes in the steam room.* As irrational as it is to promise a reward you can give yourself anyway, the enticement usually works.

The steam room is twelve feet long and six feet wide, easily measured by counting the tile. The only splotch of color is the worn sleeve of a five-foot length of ragged green garden hose attached to a faucet. The timer is broken so you have to spray the thermostat sensor above the door. If you put your finger over the nozzle it produces enough pressure to sustain a spray that will reach the sensor. If you hold it there long enough, sometimes up to a full sixty seconds, the pipes, which are imprisoned in a casing of cedar slats, begin a slow deep gurgle. The gurgles grow into tapping, and the tapping becomes a shhh-shhh swishing, and finally thick clouds of steam escape from between the slats of cedar. In seconds the small white cell is filled with such a concentration of steam that your skin cries out. I have witnessed grown men yelp like puppies and leap for the door.

An L-shaped ledge rims half the room, providing a small space to host rigorously sweating bodies. I am told women can tolerate less body space than men, but it is an observable phenomenon in the steam room that postures stiffen when too many naked males are required to sit too close to one another. I have felt my own body squeeze itself into a smaller size to gain distance from another male body as it enters my space, usurping the peace I created within my own frontiers.

The steam room is most therapeutic when I am by myself and able to lean back against the short wall, legs extended out fully along the tile ledge. Yet it only reveals its sacred nature when two or more are gathered in the midst of steam.

One other man sharing the steam room is most tolerable, so long as he does not shave or perform exercises. There are such offenders. One of the regulars is Frodo, a meticulous middle-aged man who seems far too concerned with keeping his body youthful and elegant.

When I open the door of the steam room and through the clouds can make out the silhouette of Frodo doing naked sit-ups on the ledge, I am overcome with despair. Equally disturbing is when I am under the covers of hot vapor and Estefan enters. His lush white mustache curves upward in a smile as the cheap metal from a disposable blue razor makes the irksome noise of scraping whiskers to the moist fungal floor. Perhaps in their respective spheres, Frodo and Estefan are fine human beings, but in the steam room they are unwelcome vermin.

Wilson is a different story.

Monday and Wednesday I gleefully share the steam room with Wilson who brings a small beaker of Eucalyptus oil to pour liberally between the slats of cedar. Few others (apart from Wilson and me) tolerate the pungent, sinus liquefying intensity of the plant. Wilson was a rapper who said the oil compensated for the cigars he smoked when he was in Atlanta or NYC cutting music deals.

The steam room is an endangered habitat.

Even as you read these smuggled stories whispered from the walls of a sacred place, a major renovation is underway at the Robert L. Cohen Center, fondly known by members as "The COE." It is unclear what will happen to the steam room. Will it be restored or eliminated? Or if it is simply torn apart and put back together, will its sacred magic seep out and leave behind an ordinary steam room? A damp chilling fog of anxiety has crept into my heart for which this steam room chronicle is my therapy.

Chapter Two

Sex with an Angel

Two naked men entered the room, one assaulted the silence with ceaseless chatter about Nikes, best brands of cellphones, and soccer Polos while the other followed behind, head bowed. Vapor poured out of the cedar slats surrounding the steam pipe and moist heat scorched my neck and arms as I tuned the dial in my head to the man doing all the talking. He neither slowed nor moderated his speech even though I was there in the corner leaning against the wall. Whether he was too engrossed in his own story to notice my presence, or indifferent, never became clear.

He spoke about his former cocaine habit and something about the words he used made me suspect the other man was also a member of their anonymous order of recovery. The storyteller still had the cadence and manic-mannerisms of cocaine-induced hyperactivity, and the velocity of his words were ratcheting. Listening to a modern-day Grimm's Fairy Tale with the steam an ephemeral and magical mist, I was carried into a new dimension. I listened, and soon the storyteller painted such graphic visual images that I hovered in the corner of the story's location like a spying specter.

No names were ever mentioned so in my head I called him Griff. It matched his gravelly, raspy voice that also fit the lifestyle he described. Griff was in his late twenties or early thirties, with a thick, tightly sculpted upper body. I don't remember a tattoo but it seemed to me he must have had several.

Griff told his silent companion about the genesis of his fall, or at least the precipice over which he dropped: The death of his parents came suddenly, both dead from an automobile accident leaving him an only child, orphaned in his early twenties and the sole recipient of their modest estate. He sold their house and belongings, liquefied whatever investments they had, and then stood triumphantly upon a pile of half a million dollars. Although Griff did not move into a bigger apartment he did quit his job and adjourned to his bed.

For months and months, he told his silent companion, he did not cross the threshold of the apartment. He ordered cocaine from a trusted companion predating the demise of his parents, to be delivered by prostitute. In this way he engaged his mind and body in a concurrent influx and outflow of vigorous pleasure, fibrillating the centers of ecstasy at least twice a day. In between prostitutes he called his favorite phone sex operators.

As Griff regaled his friend with a litany

describing the disembodied voices, each with their own name and special abilities, my thoughts stuttered over the notion of a favorite phone sex operator and what fantasized sexual intimacy actually is. It seemed a simple math problem I should be able to compute, but I couldn't quite figure it out.

I tuned back into Griff who was extolling his companion about his amazing life. He lived on Chinese food and pizza, often delivered along with his cocaine. If he needed groceries or alcohol he had them delivered as well. Within the walls of his domicile he was King of the Wild Things, and this made him exceedingly pleased. His happiness and contentment seemed impossibly complete and month after month he slept, ate, drank, tooted and cavorted without discovering his fill.

Somewhere, the occasion or day was not marked in his memory, a nagging thought broke through his bliss. Though he was able to keep it on the other side of the apartment door for a very long time, eventually the thought became a home invasion. There would come a time when he would run out of money.

Griff's voice sank and mellowed. He no longer reminisced in the afterglow of his Caligula lifestyle. Sometime in the early part of December he remembered calculating that the money would run out near Christmas.

Now his voice became steely and resolute: he would not allow the inevitability of scarcity to diminish the pleasures of his current life, but even so, he did begin making preparations for that day. He made certain he had all the supplies required, and sifted through thoughts about who he would want to see and talk with when the day finally arrived.

The day came on December 24th. It was Christmas Eve, and like all the other days in his three-room palace he had no memory of the weather outside. A Zen-like focus now trained his every sense on the present moment inside his apartment where he was about to abdicate the throne he inhabited for, what suddenly seemed, too short a reign.

The crescendo of his prodigal journey arrived, he told his friend with a flat voice echoing a deep sense of resignation. From his perch on the top of his kingdom he could look out and see the prospect of coming down after being high for months and months. He could envision being alone without any money to pay for companionship. The inevitable homelessness that would arrive abruptly and painfully when there was no longer any money whatsoever was a hot breath in his face. Surveying the landscape from his throne that bled kingdom, power and glory by the minute, he resolved to kill himself.

Late on Christmas Eve, as the world around him hovered in hushed anticipation of a dawning joy, Griff entered the solace of his favorite prostitute. When she was gone, only then did he enjoy the Mongolian Beef and

Crab Rangoon wrapped in the plastic smiley-face bag tied with a soiled red ribbon. Full for the last time, he climbed into his bed, slid between the covers on his back, ingested the last of his cocaine and with one arm hugging a freshly loaded shotgun like it was his soft and shapely Moll, Griff used his other hand to reach for the phone.

He dialed the phone sex line and smiled meekly at the sound of Angie's soft voice. Griff, grim and maudlin in his nearing sobriety, told Angie good-bye. She asked him what was the matter. The conversation drilled deep into the night, Angie talked him down and encouraged him to get help. With amazing resourcefulness she found Griff the local crisis hotline and in the face of his steep resistance, finally got him to agree to a conference call: Griff, Angie, and some anonymous hotline volunteer who went home that night with a story to tell. In the end, she saved his life. Angie, he said, was his Guardian Angel whom God had sent him at the critical moment to preserve his life.

• • •

The hot gaseous cloud was so thin that the horrid white light glared against the whiter tile, so I closed my eyes and pretended Griff and his companion didn't see me. I contemplated the paradox of a phone sex operator as an angel.

There were so many questions I wanted to ask, but I was an eavesdropper, a total stranger listening in on a miraculous story of recovery. Clearly Griff found footholds into the Twelve Steps and was making it, even if only one day at a time. So who was I to tell Griff that God doesn't rescue some people as if a cosmic Prince Charming while allowing a billion others to starve to death? Even though snarled thoughts yelled at each other agitating my brain, I also felt a breathless awe in the face of such serendipity.

Suddenly my brain cleared as all but one thought fell from my head onto the dingy floor: *Griff's moment of metamorphosis is natural, more natural than miraculous.*

He described his Christmas Eve epiphany as a spiral down and a stripping away of all the things that kept him from recovery. One by one, that which kept him from stillness disappeared; one by one, that which kept him from himself disappeared; one by one, that which numbed him disappeared. The moment of life or death crystallized everything and then, in that horrid moment, he could feel there was a spark of life left to live for.

At that very moment Griff and his companion decided to leave. The glass door that drips in perpetual sweat slowly closed behind them before their absence even registered.

"Wait!" I wanted to yell, as if I had some

right to hear or know more than I already did about the life of a total stranger. Still, I did not break in uninvited. Griff was the one who crossed my boundary, and he was the one who took my attention hostage with the force of his story. But suddenly I was the one left wanting more, alone again in the steam room.

I leaned down and grabbed the end of the worn green hose, aimed it toward the broken thermostat above the door, and turned the faucet handle. The spray hit its target and within seconds the clanging of pipes issued a new cloud of steam that grew so thick the walls and door disappeared. At that very moment Frodo opened the door. He sat down and immediately began his annoying exercises, the small of his back making suction noises with every sit-up. I left with a grimace in my stomach but forced myself to mumble, "Mornin'."

The cool air of the shower area shocked my skin as the door closed behind me.

Chapter Three

The Devolution of Ego

I wasn't a priest for very long, but that is what my mother calls me. She could never accept that I left the Catholic Church to become a *Protestant* minister. Despite what she says about not keeping it in my pants, I wasn't defrocked for some sexual indiscretion. I fell in love with a woman and we wanted to get married, and by then I was already having difficulty with the doctrinalism of the Roman Catholic Church. What I didn't know then was that my trajectory wouldn't change and, before too many years, my adopted denomination would also begin to be too tight a fit as well.

Like a tire wobbling off its wheel, the Protestant collar came off too. The anxieties of my parishioners and the inability of the hierarchy to see holy ground beyond the borders of their own institution was a daily slog through a fetid swamp of black mud. Getting a real job without weekend hours and nobody measuring the purity of my life was sweet liberation. Still, the steam room calls me back to those times like nothing else.

It was late on a Friday morning;

primetime for an empty steam room.

As usual, my workout was light and even though it was the heart of winter in Buffalo I was sweating profusely. My favorite towel was wrapped around my waist, a solid purple beach towel so old the terry was worn to strips of thread in places, then I slammed the locker door, pinched the combination lock, and walked toward the sanctuary. As I turned the corner thick clouds of vapor through the steam room door appeared in my view. *Who was in there?*

I opened and closed the door in a hurry so not to diminish the room at its peak of intensity. The outline of a body was visible from the corner of my eye as I passed and took a seat on the bench at the far end of the room. It's *"The Thinker,"* I said to myself, but then realized he was far more slumped than the muscular man of art.

This Thinker was more of a pouter. His chin cupped the palms of both hands and stubby fingertips covered his eyes. As much as I could see through the fog, his eyes appeared to be closed and the weight of his upper body foisted upon his elbows. He seemed oblivious to my presence even though I was keenly aware of his.

Sitting across from the cedar-encased pipes, just above the faucet and green garden hose, I had as much distance from The Thinker as possible. My back was against the hot, moist wall and legs extended fully along the tiled ledge. I closed my eyes and immediately felt the compelling desire for sleep, and gradually drifted into that lovely netherworld where the sands of wakefulness are gently combed by the rhythmic waves of sleep.

"I thought I was supposed to be great," is all he said.

Is he talking to me? Just in case, I answered, "Beg pardon?"

He didn't answer, leaving me to straddle the awkward moment and wonder if he'd heard me. I started to wonder anxiously if I made up his voice in my head. My mouth was opened in mid-flight to beg his pardon again when he spoke.

"I always thought I was supposed to be important," he continued, "you know what I mean?" But without waiting for my response he kept talking.

"Back in the day (which was only the first of his many annoying colloquialisms), I was in the thick of things. You know, the 60's. Man, we just knew we were changing the world in those days."

"Yeah ... I wish we had," I inserted, though I don't think he heard me.

"I was in Ann Arbor, man; that was where it was at. Did you know it all came from Ann Arbor? Yeah, that's right," he exclaimed as if I was surprised. "It started in the Midwest and went to each coast. Hah! It started in the freakin' Midwest. Can you believe that? Today it starts in some goddamn marketing asshole's conference room and spreads like a beetle infestation through the Internet and television. But what do they spread? Bullshit. Consumerism. Fucking materialistic bullshit engorging adolescent desires."

"Yeah," I said, weakly.

This felt awkward. Normally, if this were one of my buddies trash-talking the culture, I would be cheerleading, the loudest voice in the Amen Corner. But something was not right. I had a feeling. One extravert to another, this guy was not actually saying what he was thinking. Uneasy now, I instinctively created distance in case this guy turned out to be a loony.

"Nah, but it's not that," he drifted off. "Maybe all the shit going on around me has something to do with it, but I think it came from somewhere else. I really did think I was supposed to be important."

Silence.

I began to think that was it, just another weird snippet of conversation from the steam room that will circulate in my brain like cell phone conversations bounce around for eternity in outer space.

Sometimes I daydream about being ninety-three and in the Alzheimer's Unit of some dilapidated nursing home, and abruptly I'll break out into steam room stories without any context, and the hapless attendant will figure my mutterings are just the dementia instead of real life stories. Or worse, those around me will think the oddments from other people's lives I moan on about are from my life. Just thinking about what I have heard and the fragments of strange lives that may come out of my mouth fills me with anticipatory embarrassment.

"No, I think it was my mother," The Thinker blurts. "Yes, I think she must have fitted me for expectations much greater than my natural size. I'm gonna call my brothers to confirm it. They are older so they must have experienced the same thing. Only ... only I can't put my finger on a single memory when my mother told me I was supposed to be important ..."

Clearly I was superfluous in this conversation. Then the dude slipped into the soup of memory, which often happens while sitting within the fog of the steam room. But his strange soliloquy pushed me up against my own memory and I felt myself twisting around to look inside, my own face now smashed up against the invisible veil between the outer and the inner.

I could see a little boy sitting in a sailboat made out of a large orange crate, a push broom handle for a mast and a torn white sheet for a sail. There he was in the middle of the back yard surrounded by an ocean of green grass, a trusty brown and white mutt curled up next to him, two castaways on the ocean of imagination. Peering through the glass of time, I feel love well up inside me for that little boy. Or maybe it is just empathy for his loneliness.

Why is that little boy so lonely? There is a gnawing knot of sadness rooted inside him and even though he is me, I can't quite put my finger on why he is so hauntingly lonely.

Perhaps all childhood is lonely, but looking at that little boy, I can't help but wonder why there is no one for him to play with. I marvel at how resigned he seems to sail by himself forever. How did that little boy become so solitary so very young?

"I used to think it was something else, you know?"

I didn't know how long I had been gone but The Thinker sounded like he thought we had been conversing intently for hours.

"I had these posters of great men in my room when I was a teenager. They were the eyes of the past looking down on me in anticipation of what I would bring to the gallery. One was an elegant glossy print my parents brought me from a trip to England, it was of St. George slaying the dragon in 17th century Realism. The animal's scales dripped with blood and the black soot of its fire stained the knight's armor. Another museum print was of Napoleon looking regal in starched uniform, expressionless with his hand tucked between the breast buttons of his coat. There were others adorning the walls of my room and I wonder now ... oh, I don't know."

Then he fell back into the abyss.

But I knew where he went. I've pressed my face so hard against the glass of memory before that I fell down the shaft until all light disappeared. It is like swimming in a dunk tank in the dark, no, more like a river. Memory is a river with unforeseen eddies that can pull you under and maybe that's what dementia is – drowning in the river while still alive.

There he was again. The Thinker bobbed up to the surface.

"I think I thought I was supposed to change the world like they did. Weren't we all going to do that? We were on deck, for Christ's sake. We were supposed to change the world like they did. I was supposed to change the world. You see, I was supposed to be more important than I turned out to be. I didn't change the world at all. Maybe I made it worse."

"No, you can't go there." It just came out, a burp of thought too buoyant to be repressed.

I realized I had been engaged in a running conversation with this stranger in my own head whether or not he actually was talking to me. Suddenly it was out in the open and I could feel my cheeks redden. So now there was nothing to do but finish it.

"Nobody carries the world on their own

shoulders. Besides, it's the little things that matter in the end, not the big ones."

"How d'ya figure?" he asked with unexpected curiosity.

"It's the accumulation of little things, over time, that make the difference. Even those few who do really big things, really great things, like Martin Luther King, Jr. or Nelson Mandela, they're only able to do them when the opportunity arrives because they have been doing the little things all along the way. You see what I mean?"

He didn't say anything so I thought I lost him; more likely it drove him into retreat as he realized he was opening his whole life to an utter stranger.

"It's like drops of rain," I added, unable to stop myself. It was as if someone put a quarter in my jukebox. "You know, droplets splashing with very little impact on a river. But the accumulation of those drops can swell the river and overflow its banks and change the course of the river forever. It's the little things, all of us together doing the little things, that make history."

"I dunno. I wish I could be sure ..." And then he shut up again.

Suddenly he stood up and left.

In an instant he was gone and I was jolted into the realization that the steam was gone too; the sterile light washed the white tile in merciless fluorescence.

I was in an empty room, just me sitting

there like that little boy in the back yard.

My shoulders slumped, I felt their weight even as I reach to turn on the spigot and spray the sensor. The rising steam lifted my spirits, heat drew moisture from every pore. Random hot droplets zinged me from the ceiling, stinging my head and shoulders.

What made that guy leave all of a sudden? The son of a bitch stirred up all these questions and this ghostly loneliness sat in the pit of my stomach like bad meatloaf. I thought my answer to his musings was pretty good.

Then again the loneliness unnerved me. His question seemed to have penetrated my happy little answer and now I felt my confidence evaporating. It is always easier to believe against someone than it is to stand naked in the open air and have your beliefs exposed and vulnerable.

Maybe he was right, we were supposed to change the world but we didn't. Maybe I was supposed to be important too, but I'm not. Maybe the accumulation of all the small things we do just doesn't stack up against the big splashy good deeds that change the world and are so much more measurable than anything I had ever done.

Still, I wanted to believe in the little things.

I wanted to believe that all those little ordinary moments echoed deep into the future even more than the cannonball splashes of spectacular events that few people can ever replicate. Some people might read this and think me neurotic as hell, but sifting through little memories puts flesh on ghosts from the past.

The Thinker raised all these questions, spread chaos in my stomach and then just up and left. Bastard. But then sometimes the steam room is like that – a promising little sprout is abruptly snuffed out. I went back to the glass of memory where I could see that little boy and wonder about why we are so lonely.

Chapter Four

Ghost Story

It was a Wilson day. The thought brought a smile even as I descended the stairs from the basketball court to the locker room. It took roughly twenty-seven seconds to shed my clothes in a pile before my locker, grab a towel and head toward the steam room.

All life was sucked out of me when Hamm was the first thing I saw after pulling open the door. Hamm is a nudist, I'd bet fifty dollars on it.

There are all kinds of people in this world, and nearly every one of them has a representative in the men's locker room at The COE. There are men who slump in their nakedness like someone forced to go out in the rain without a coat, knowing they'll be drenched whether they walk or run. The shoulders of such men slump forward and round down, their arms hang limp at either side and they walk with dread, their gait something between a shuffle and baby steps.

Other men are driven by a shy modesty, and flock to corner lockers where they can arrange their clothing so everything can be taken off and put on without ever turning around. If they shower at all, these men bring a robe or wear a towel and allow for as little airtime as possible. I am told the women's locker room has shower stalls for privacy, but our showers, like most men's locker rooms, are in one open coliseum.

Then there are the peacocks who strut. They don't just get undressed and shower, they prolong every movement of the locker room symphony by stretching naked in the aisle where others have to walk around them, stand naked at the sink while shaving and brushing teeth, lean naked against a locker while engaged in prolonged conversations even with those who might be fully dressed, or sit naked on the bench reading a book.

I have witnessed such men standing near another man who was getting dressed while spreading apart every fold and crevice of their body as they used a box fan on the floor like a blow dryer. Mind you, these are not all replicas of Greek gods. Fat, thin, muscular or sagging – none is an indicator, nor is the size of their junk. So perhaps they are not strutting at all. They may simply be indifferent about public nakedness. Even so, their very indifference to how others around them may feel reveals a disturbing degree of self-orbit.

The majority of men in the locker room just get it done with a degree of normalcy that draws no attention. Maybe they too experience the whole range of feelings from embarrassed and awkward to precious and preening but their body language is more utilitarian. They just get dressed.

I read somewhere that St. Augustine was catapulted into his reflection that would eventually curse Western Civilization with the notion of "Original Sin," because of an erection one afternoon in the public baths. He wanted to know why his body would do something his mind didn't want it to do, and eventually, through some twisted rationalizing contemplation, he arrived at the explanation of original sin through Adam and Eve. That is probably not the first time a hard-on changed the course of human history.

Hamm is a strutter. He doesn't just sit in the steam room, he *lounges* in it. Somehow on that narrow bench of tile he seems to flop and spread out as if it were a Lazy Boy recliner. Thank God he doesn't exercise and stretch the way Frodo does, if he did it would be unbearable.

When I entered the steam room Hamm was already well ensconced, lodged in his usual repose in the far corner across from the cedar slats. I took up a station in the corner by the door where I leaned against one wall and extend my legs so my feet nearly touched the opposing wall. Not quite settled, the door opened. *Wilson*!

Wilson is huge. He touches both sides of the door as he wedges through, but as big as he is, his presence is far more accommodating than Hamm's. Immediately, as the door opened and the room darkened under his shadow, I knew instinctively these two had not yet crossed paths.

Moving with unusual grace for someone so large, Wilson stepped directly toward the cedar slats covering the steam pipes opposite to where Hamm was lounging. I watched, and a grin stretched my lips from ear to ear in anticipation of Hamm's reaction to the piercing invigoration of steam laced with Eucalyptus oil.

The tiny amber bottle was nearly invisible in the massive mitt of Wilson's hand as he dripped the fragrant liquid onto the steaming slats. Hamm's sprawl was fully uncoiled because he hadn't bothered to open his eyes. I pivoted and put my feet on the floor to offer plenty of room for Wilson as he sat down matter-of-factly between Hamm and me. Immediately the pungent oil escaped on the vapors of steam and Hamm's eyes widened from slits to half dollars. It was almost like a Loony Tunes cartoon. In the time it took to breathe twice, Hamm was through the door and slamming it shut on us.

"Pussy," Wilson muttered as laughter shook both our bellies.

I felt the kind of perverse glee that squeezes out any kinder sense of propriety, like when someone falls in a particularly awkward way. The fact it shouldn't be funny makes the laughter all the more urgent.

It was never funny when my mother used

to laugh at me, and so the decay of that deep stinging cavity caused a slight wisp of empathy for Hamm to rise up within me. She used to cackle when I fell or failed, and then again later when she told her friends about how I had done something stupid.

I have memories of standing drenched in humiliation, a withering fern pelted by hail. Mother with her friends, balancing a cigarette between painted fingernails in one hand and playing cards fanned in the other, all of them laughing at her Stupid Kid Stories while I served ice to refresh their daytime cocktails.

"So there was this Irish priest," Wilson said, "who was leading a class or Bible study or something like dat."

Wilson had moved down to the corner where Hamm had been sitting and I was still at the opposite corner near the door. Wilson was a high school football star who had a scholarship offer to play at Ohio State, but he blew out his knee helping at a football camp the summer after his senior year. Inside that massive round body was a football player's strength and muscle. He had a giant animal claw tattoo creeping up his neck because that was his moniker back in high school: *Claw*.

I looked at him and tried to imagine how he fit on the ledge, wondering how much of his weight was held up by those tree stump legs because he overflowed the tiled bench. He was wearing his ever-present black doo-rag and one of those sweat bags, the kind of material that doesn't breathe so it can hold all the body heat inside: a sweat bag within a steam room.

I've seen him sit in the steam room with his whole body wrapped inside some article of clothing except his feet. When he does that I find myself involuntarily leaning hard against the far wall in case he explodes.

"He asks 'em, 'How many of you believe in ghooosts?' and they all raised their hands."

To my surprise and utter delight, Wilson had perfected an Irish brogue and it made me guffaw.

"The priest, he's surprised and asks 'em again, 'So how many of you have had an actual *experience* wit a ghooost?' Well, the priest is surprised again as they all raise their hands."

Again, his brogue is spot-on, and to hear it coming out of Wilson is a bloody rip.

"Okay then, how many of you have ever had a *sexual* experience wit a ghooost?"

Now we both laugh.

"One guy in the back of the room raises his hand. 'Timothy O'Toole, you've had a *sexual* experience wit a ghooost?'"

Then Wilson paused. He looked at me with a half-smile curled up one cheek and adds, "'Ooh, sorry Fadder, I t'ought you said *goooat.*'"

Tears streamed down my face and I choked for air. We were so raucous that Estefan opened the door and looked in to see what was going on. Neither one of us could stop laughing long enough to answer his curious look so he walked away and the door closed.

I was still chuckling when Estefan opened the door again, this time with a plastic blue razor in his hand and stroking his neck as natural as a bird landing to perch on a wire.

"Why you gotta shave in here, man?" Wilson asked, his face curled into a quizzical smile that moves so much flesh around that his eyes become little slits that frown. I cheered inside.

"Why- why- why I don't have to if you find it disturbing." Estefan stuttered his response in the formal little way he has of speaking.

"Good," Wilson retorts, "now put that goddamn thing down."

Estefan dropped the razor on the floor, his hand visibly shaking. I picked it up and handed it to him feeling only slightly guilty to be relishing the moment of victory a la Wilson.

"You believe in ghosts?" I asked Wilson.

"Now you talking," he smiled. "I don't just believe in them, I seen 'em."

"When?" Even as I asked it, I could see Estefan was unable to take his eyes off Wilson and he appeared to have stopped breathing. I felt myself trying to stifle another chuckle.

"My auntie was dying. She was up in 'The General'," he said, referring to Buffalo

General Hospital. "She was in bed dying for a long time. One day I walked in and she's just smiling away, and looking all goofy like."

"Was she talking to anyone?" I asked.

"No, she's just laying there on her back, oxygen tube in her nose, eyes all wide and watering. But she's smiling. So I says, 'Auntie, what you smiling at?' and she holds up her skinny old hand like it was a fifty pound weight, and points a long boney finger to the end of the bed."

"What did you see, Mr. Wilson," Estefan asked and we both looked at him with astonishment.

"Well ... I didn't see nothing at first. I leaned down and got real close to Auntie and asked her, 'Who ya see, Auntie?' She smiled even bigger, and then she whispers in a teeny tiny little voice, 'Him.'"

Estefan and I freeze, our butts hanging on the edge of the tile bench.

"Sure enough, there was my uncle. His face was hanging there real big, about twice the size it shoulda been and his body all swirly like. 'Uncle!' I shout and poof, he disappears."

"Uh oh," I said.

"Yeah, 'uh oh' is right. Auntie looked back at me and her eyes were flashing. Man, if looks could kill they'd have taken me out on a gurney. She died later that night, peaceful as could be."

The three of us sat in silence and I imagined, like me, they thought about seeing ghosts and loved ones who died and then suddenly noticed the pipes had stopped clanging. I was thinking about spraying the thermostat again but instead turned to Estefan.

"You ever seen a ghost?"

"Why no, I shouldn't think so, no," he said in his usual nervous fashion. He's like that, nervous as a dog that's been beaten.

"What about you, Big Man," Wilson asked. "You ever saw'd a ghost before?"

"Not just one, but a whole crowd of them."

"Don't be laying down bullshit now," Wilson warned me, "cause I know my ghost stories and I'll know if you're talking shit."

"It was after my dad died, about ten years ago. My brothers and sisters and I had been cleaning out his house for a week to get it ready to sell, and sorting stuff, you know. Well, one night I got it into my mind to go down to the little church where we grew up. I don't know why I hankered to do something like that because that church holds no good memories for me."

"It's cause you do stupid things when you're grieving," Wilson said authoritatively.

"Yeah, suppose so. Anyway, we grew up in this rinky-dink little town out in the middle of Indiana, name of Dunkirk. There was nothing to do at night for a grown man, or anyone else for that matter, so I went on down to the church and it was open. They still don't lock their doors at night in Dunkirk, or at least they didn't ten years ago."

"They'd be finding dead bodies all 'round if that was Buffalo." Wilson chuckled and Estefan sniffed assent.

"So I went in and turned on a dimmer switch, keeping the lights kind of low. It's a little church that seats maybe a hundred. It's long and narrow like a bowling alley with old dark-wood pews on each side, and an aisle down the middle. The pews have dusty red cushions on them and the whole place smells musty like old forgotten books. It was night so I couldn't see the stained glass windows that captured me as a kid, you know, coke bottle thick pieces of cobalt blue, plush red, amber gold, turquoise and amethyst. I sat down in the second from the last row and just stayed real quiet."

Estefan cleared his little voice and said, "Volumes have been written about apparitions that populate the old churches of the United Kingdom."

I thought he was about to continue his lecture but Wilson injected, "Shut up, fool, let the man go on."

"Well, so, I just sat there for a really long time and started to get the feeling I wasn't alone. The hairs on the back of my neck stood up and chills ran down my spine. I mean like *real* chills, as if someone was dripping ice water out of an eyedropper on each vertebrae. I didn't really believe in ghosts at the time, and I didn't want to leave the church, and so I spoke up."

"Man, you courtin' trouble if you be talkin' directly to a ghost, don't you know that!" Wilson shrunk back as if repulsed at the thought.

"Well nothing happened. I just told them I didn't want any trouble and I had only come to say goodbye to my dad who had been praying at that little church his whole life. Then, and I don't know what made me think of it, I decided to sing."

"What!" Wilson was incredulous at this news. "Man, you got balls singin' to ghosts."

"Did you choose an 18th or 19th century hymn?" Estefan wanted to know.

"I don't know when it was written! I reached for a hymnal as I stood up, and as I did the book just happened to open to an old familiar tune, 'For All the Saints.' So I started singing it. I don't know exactly what hit me but it landed deep in the gut. I could feel tears backing up behind my eyes and then they started rolling down my cheeks. I didn't want to crack up so I sang with as full a voice as I could, even though my words were wavering. After the second verse it started to happen."

"You're creeping me out, man." Wilson edged up against the wall as I went on.

"I saw movement down in the front pews. It was swirly and cloudy and I could barely see it at first. But the more I sang the clearer the images became. They were all down there in the front pews, and I got the impression they were singing with me. There must have been a dozen or so, but it was all too murky to make out any details. When I finished the last verse, and there are eight verses to that hymn, they all turned around and faced me. I think, but maybe only imagined it, they were applauding."

I looked at Wilson and he was staring at Estefan. I turn my head to glance at Estefan and he was looking nervously at Wilson. No one said anything for a moment.

"Whew!" Wilson let out a huge sigh of relief. "I thought they was going to attack you. That's a righteous story, Big Man."

Something about Wilson calling me "big" is both pleasing and confusing, but I am glad my story reached the same dramatic level as his. We both looked at Estefan for a moment, as if to urge him on, but simultaneously thought better of it.

Wilson never stays in the steam room very long; small wonder given all he wears. He waved us off and left, followed almost immediately by Estefan. I was left alone to think about ghosts and death, and to remember my dad.

I was not ready to leave so I sprayed the thermostat and washed down the ledge before lying down full length on my back. There was peace in the steam room, surrounded as I was by quiet and filled with better memories.

I closed my eyes to lower myself gently

into the moment. I thought about how many people I knew who actually believed in heaven and hell or some kind of afterlife. Reincarnation is big these days. I have tried to imagine it but can't get very far. It seems like all such theories are only a means to make us feel better about our ignorance or give us a sense that the scales of justice will balance at the end.

Shit! I heard myself say inside my head as the moment deflated. Hamm pushed the door open, flopped down on the bench and let out a staccato of machine gun mutterings.

"What the hell was that stuff? Who is that guy? I'm reporting him to management. What kind of an asshole would pour toxic, smelly-ass shit into the steam pipes?"

Hamm spewed his non-stop litany of complaints as I got up and left. I crossed over to the large open cavity across from the steam room, rimmed by a dozen showerheads and body soap dispensers. The cooler shower water crashed over my head rinsing the glow of sweat off my body before I lathered up, rinsed again, and half-heartedly dried off.

Even then, passing in front of the steam room on my way to the locker, Hamm was still muttering to himself inside a shroud of steam. I stopped and sat on the bench just outside to air dry for a moment, but really it was just to pause.

The voice in my head muttered too, but about memories and ghosts, and the thoughts that whisper of a past that is always hovering and begs to be heard. In spite of Hamm and the sound of his grunts and groans, I felt a kind of awe that in the envelope of the steam room these vestiges of the sacred could be found among the strange and peculiar stories left there. I suspected that somehow even Hamm contributed to its sacredness. Somehow.

Chapter Five

A World Full of Bastards

Dweedle sat on the bench every morning after his swim. At seventy-five or older he still swam every day of the week. Arriving at the crack of dawn when the gym opens, he is sitting there when I arrive at a more civilized hour. He sits with his naked ass on the wooden bench reading *The Buffalo News* word-for-word until he's gotten "his money's worth," he says.

It was shoes that brought Dweedle and me together, so to speak.

He had extraordinarily big feet for someone his size, disproving the rumor about the ratio of foot length to penis. I have big feet too, so Dweedle took it upon himself to help me find better shoes. But before the advent of our accidental big-dog solidarity, there were only two things Dweedle ever said to me – no matter that our lockers were only a few doors apart.

The more genteel utterance began with Dweedle wheezing a laugh between his teeth, followed by finger tapping on the newsprint of the comic page, and a gleam in the eye as he muttered, "That Dennis the Menace, he's a corker."

The other phrase was evoked when I asked him if there is any good news in the world today. My query always, at any time and on any day, produced the same response: "They're no fuckin' good. The Bastards are no fuckin' good." Some days I asked him the question just so I could hear him say it in that peculiar Buffalonian brogue that is one part New Yorker, one part Midwesterner, and one part Canadian.

I've been told with authority that Dweedle was a "bag man" for the Republicans back in his younger years. Apparently he went to jail sometime in the 50's or 60's as the fall guy in one of the perennial corruption cycles that plague Buffalo and New York State. All I really know is that he keeps a gun in his locker and thinks the world is full of bastards that are no fucking good.

It took me awhile to feel affection for a prickly guy like Dweedle, but over the years he's grown on me. Now he's like the paper on the stoop in the morning, or the barista behind the counter whose perky smile or smartass greeting sets the planet in its proper orbit.

When Dweedle had a heart attack last year and was gone for several months, it was as if the music had died in the locker room. At the noon hour, when basketball regulars or lunchtime runners were getting their armor on, banter was thick and the music of aging machismo reached its perfect pitch. But in the morning, the locker room depended upon Dweedle's gruff baritone just to lift it to tolerable.

On that particular morning, Dweedle was nowhere to be found, and it was just me and a different old man in the steam room. He was older than Dweedle and, like most of the steam room regulars, I didn't know his real name. In my head I called him "Bull," because it described his short, thick body with bandy legs and generally gruff demeanor.

Even though Bull was over eighty, if he could have done away with the crooked gate of his walk by having a hip replacement or something, he might have passed for late sixties. Compared to Dweedle, Bull was a spring chicken. I've seen that old man do one-armed push-ups and I'm guessing he was a Leatherneck by his ramrod posture and buzz cut.

Bull did not normally talk to me; in fact he didn't even acknowledge my presence when I entered the steam room that morning. So the sound of his voice directed at me through the fog was disconcerting.

He began by comparing recent stock market activity with the woe induced by the crash of 1929 and I wondered what I had done wrong to be subjected to an economics lecture so early in the morning. Bull, sitting with both feet planted firmly on the slimy tile of the steam room floor, spoke in his usual low staccato voice that seemed to leak out one corner of his pencil-line lips. He said his father lost a million dollars in one day – and then he added, "That was when a million dollars was real money."

He said he remembered people coming to the door asking for bread or a sandwich. "And it wasn't just one person coming to your door in a single day, but five, six or seven of them almost every day."

There was a bitter awe resonant in his voice as if talking about a devastating storm, but he was talking about people he knew back in those bad old days when he was only eight years old, friends of his family who held high positions in business but ended up riding the rails in search of forgetfulness. "Not like now," he said, as if the recent recession was a trifle. But then he told me about something else.

Bull said that months before the stock market went south at the end of the George W. years, he told his financial advisor that events were starting to remind him of those dark days before the Great Depression. He asked his advisor if maybe he shouldn't put his stocks into bonds or something else safer. His advisor said he could do that but he didn't recommend it.

"The market will go back up eventually," his advisor offered in the way those people do, believing their own formulas and prognostication like a meteorologist glibly forecasts sunshine.

"But I'm 87," the old man reminded his advisor. "I don't have 10 or 20 years to wait for it to come back if it crashes."

Nevertheless, he took the advisor's professional suggestion and left his stocks alone.

"I lost $200,000 goddamn dollars in one day," he grumbled.

That sent him hurtling down memory lane. Suddenly he was reminiscing vaguely about a run-in he had once with "the Commies." He actually said, "Commies." It was a surreal moment and I wanted to pinch myself to make sure I hadn't fallen into a movie.

It was difficult to make out the exact nature of the conflict he described but it seemed to have been a public political struggle of some kind, just after WWII. There is no way I can replicate what he told me, but it was something about being in a debate with "the Commies" and how he lost the argument, and how the memory of that public failure was still with him like a bullet lodged so close to the spine it can't be removed.

All of this was only a prelude to confession.

Bull bellowed his hatred of Socialism and Communism, as if they were wolves scratching at the door. Then he said, his face ashen, he was now ready to admit some kind of regulations had to be put on those "greedy bastards" on Wall Street.

The poor guy told me all about the business he had, and about when he retired twenty years earlier and got screwed out of a large chunk of savings. He said that at sixty-seven he sold his business, but because of something his accountants had not done properly, he ended up owing over $300,000 in state and federal taxes. Then two of his three children died. He seamlessly laced this grim news in with the loss of his life's savings.

I could hardly breathe. This old guy, who looked like he was cut from stone and spoke with a voice so rigid any other noise bounced off it, had been violently stuffed with grief and misery. One child died of cancer and the other from a heart attack.

It was not yet 10:30 AM and Bull was rolling out a litany of sorrow that I picked up and held with him. He described each sorrowful event with the same terse speech that wraps any residual grief like butcher paper can only thinly conceal the blood of raw meat.

My mind wandered to his bandy legs. I wondered if the grief he carried simply bowed those sturdy trunks. Then he let out a loud "harrumph" and I suddenly saw myself sitting there with my mouth gaping open. He had gotten up and gimped toward the door.

"I am sorry for your losses, sir," I said, stuttering in the way people do when searching for impossible words. "You have been through tougher times and had more losses than most people I know." The words felt awkward, cardboard cutouts when flesh and blood was called for.

His words, in that same low, brittle tone, skipped across the space between us like a stone on water. "It's no different than anyone else, everyone goes through it," he said. "You gotta keep going."

Those last words were a pinch softer and more striking for what was absent among them. He said it without bitterness. There was a softness that did not deny his pain but put it in perspective with everyone else's. He said it without any sense of victimization, without any sense of resentment. In the sound of his voice were the notes of resonant humility.

Standing there, one hand on the door handle, he looked down at me and right into my eyes as he said, "I try to look up at the sky and enjoy the beauty of the world and life." Then awkwardly, less comfortably, he added, "You know what I mean?"

He almost seemed embarrassed as he asked it, like he caught himself softening a little too far.

"Oh yeah, I know what you mean," I quipped with a smile. The door closed. The banging of the steam pipes started up. A hot fog enveloped me and I felt the relief of being hidden.

I fell back through time and landed in the fog of a childhood memory.

It was a November day in seventh grade and I watched my younger self running home in a frenzied panic to retrieve my Converse All-Stars and get back to school in time for a basketball game. I leapt up the front steps two at a time and through the front door that stood wide open. My stomach lurched into my throat for fear of what I would find, again.

My mother was passed out on the floor of the living room, completely naked. Her clothes appeared to have been shed randomly around the room as if dropped in the course of a stuporous dance, the furniture and knickknacks strewn in her wake. Even more horrifying was the large Chinese dragon urn normally situated to the left of the fireplace that she must have mistaken for the toilet bowl. Feces were smeared down its side and on the carpet below.

I wanted to run back out the door. I wanted to cry. I wanted to play basketball with fierce vengeance. But I did not succumb to the pull of panic or disgust and started cleaning up the mess instead. Knowing I could never erase the look on my father's face if he were to come home to that ugliness was stronger than the revulsion or anger I felt. That young boy would have done anything to save his father from more sorrow, to save himself from having to see that look on his father's face. As I watched the boy in the memory, I knew he would miss the game and, unwilling to explain the absence to his coach, he would be benched for two more games.

The memory elongates to two months later, when after a torrent of expletive-laced diatribe my young self-evoked against my mother and her drunkenness, my father figured out what had happened and how many times similar scenes had taken place. Then that look on his face was for me.

He pulled from me how much sanitizing of the scene I did that afternoon before he got home, and he insisted I describe in detail what I did to minimize the shock of each episode and why I felt the need to protect him. It was after that painful night of confessions that he sent my mother away for treatment the first time.

My then-girlfriend, Deanne, had lost her mother to colon cancer when she was eight years old. When my thoughts spun downward into the darkness of self-pity, usually a week or so after one of my mother's episodes, Deanne would remind me that at least we both had a home, food, clothes, friends, and one parent who cared for us.

"Think about Paulie Sherfick or Spud Bruce, they got no one," she would say, her words laden with sadness.

Deanne and my dad were like Bull, prying open any moment that had slammed shut on hope or happiness, and insisting I look at it from a different angle. Like a cat can be dropped upside down and will always land on its feet, Deanne and Dad could Jiu-Jitsu any event and re-frame it with opportunity and promise. That is not my instinct but they taught me it could be my strategy. It's made the difference between night and day more than once in my life and Bull reminded me of it again.

I got lost in those thoughts and zoned out. For a minute or five, I didn't really know, I got lost in thoughts and memories until a drip of hot water from the ceiling landed on the top of my ear and snapped me back from my shroud within the steam and quiet. The door opened. It was Wilson!

Wilson smiled, walked over to the cedar box and poured a couple of drops of oil onto the steam pipes. One deep breath and my sinuses opened with a cheer as the rush of eucalyptus penetrated my head and incited an explosion behind my eyes. Too bad Bull wasn't there to enjoy it.

Chapter Six

Where Preachers Go to Die

There was a man I had never seen before sitting on the short end of the L-shaped bench, so I stood waiting, looking down and expecting Hamm to move. I opened my mouth to say something just as his eyes opened. He expelled a loud sigh and, instead of making room for me to sit down, he got up and left. Jerk.

Before sitting down I reached for the hose and sprayed off any vestiges of Hamm from the bench. I looked over at the man whom I had never seen before.

"Do you mind if I start up the steam?"

"No, go ahead," he replied, then after a hesitation, "that would be nice. This place seems like it would be 'a must' in Buffalo in the winter." He chortled while speaking.

"Not from here, huh?"

"No," he said with his nose ever-so-slightly turned up, "what is that smell?"

"Eucalyptus oil," I laughed, realizing Wilson must have been here pretty early in the morning. "Does it bother you?"

"No, not at all," he said. "It reminds me of someone." I noticed him slump, and then almost crumple.

It was quiet. The steam pipes had ceased their chugging but the room was wrapped in a white cloud. No one was taking a shower outside, no banter could be heard from the locker area; we were subsumed by a loud quiet. He began to talk, haltingly in a small voice that sliced into the quiet but did not kill it right away. Through the cloud I could make out his posture and the motion of his head when he spoke, and he was speaking toward the ceiling in the corner of the room more than to me.

I did not listen at first because he was so quiet, he could even have been mumbling to himself. But when those first sharpened words hit my ears I knew what was coming – a steam room confession. I have heard them before but it never ceases to amaze me. I know bartenders and hairdressers get the same thing, a strange thinning of boundaries without the formal code of secrecy offered by a therapist or priest. I've heard more intimate confessions with less varnish in the steam room than I ever did as a priest and minister.

"Do you believe in God?" he asked me.

"I guess so ..." I said with less commitment than a dead fish. I felt the guardrails go up as they always do when talk with a stranger turns to religion.

"I'm a preacher," he began, and I caught myself suddenly looking at him carefully for the first time. I knew I wouldn't be looking so hard if he started out saying he was a plumber. As I measure the man, I decided to keep the closet door closed on my identity as a former holy man.

He looked to be average height, as far as I could tell since he was sitting down. He was average weight too, and in fact, he was an average looking middle-aged guy. I noted his rather large head with an outstanding explosion of hair that retained a sandy beach color.

I watched his demeanor change as he unwrapped his story, appearing to shrink ever further before my very eyes. The preacher bent over at the waist, his face cupped in his hands like a prisoner leaning on bars.

He told me he wasn't sure about God any more.

The tubes of my intestines immediately twisted into knots; snarled fishing line came to mind. Sardonically, with a slick of greasy oil dripping from his words, he acknowledged that in his profession ambivalence about God is fatal. I felt a nearly uncontrollable urge to back as far into the corner of the steam room as I could, then grab the hose and aim it at him like water cannon. In fact, I suddenly realized I was curled up, having unconsciously pulled my legs to my chest where I was hugging them. In my head I chastised myself for this repulsion, but still I couldn't help feeling the guy was a spiritual leper.

This was the closest to the edge he had

ever been, he said. It was an open pit he was staring into, and being so close to the edge gave him vertigo. Looking into his doubts was the last thing he wanted to do but some unseen siren stole his gaze and locked it onto the pit. He was being pulled into a serpent-headed coil of doubts in spite of his fears. The well of emptiness within him never closed, he confessed with a slight twitch of his head, and it was dark and dank; a colorless emptiness he just wanted to be gone.

I closed my eyes and tried to see colorless darkness. Nope. I saw reds and yellows and blues swirling around inside my eyelids.

"It was a burning bush," he told me, and went on to describe his first encounter with God.

"At fifteen you can imagine anything," he began, and then went on to tell me he still remembers it as if it were last Christmas. A sudden bodily feeling like no other had overtaken him: it was God inside of him. But not only that: he was in God and everything in the universe was a part of everything else in the universe. I wanted to ask if there were drugs involved but he was too earnest for humor.

But now, he said, his face drooping more than ever, the memory of God lived side by side with his more recent encounter with what he matter-of-factly called his *sin*.

God drifted away like a fallen leaf carried

to the far side of a pond, but *the sin* came flooding back with a tide of sweat and anguish. The image of her face came with it, he moaned.

Of course it was a woman.

I was hoping for something less cliché but there it was again: sex. Ministers, sex, and church are an absolute magnetic repulsion. Churches cannot deal with sex of any kind, and even when a minister's sexuality remains confined within the narrowly prescribed boundaries, it is still a taboo subject. Even a little toe outside the lines creates hysteria in the hen house.

His sin was now more real than his faith, he whispered in a parched voice. As if to prove the point he confided he could easily reach up and touch her face again within his mind's eye. In the vividness of his imagination he could look up and see the soft pink of her cheeks framed in the tunnel of her long silken hair.

Do I really want to hear this? I wanted to put my hands over my ears and shout, "Nananananaananana!"

He stared up at the corner of the room again, only with his eyes closed. His painful self-disclosure turned to titillation and it creeped me out. With a moony smile he described how her wry grin curled at the corners of her lips, and even now he could see her face as she posted up and down on the saddle of his hips.

Good God! I am going spray this guy with the hose. Really, I was going to.

His eyes still closed, and that grin still smeared across his face, he said she knew exactly what to do. He said he pretended to know what to do when he was with her, but acknowledged his body merely responded to the dance of her movements. It was all so new, so wild, and so free.

"How strange," he said, suddenly looking right at me. "My memories of God, even the most vivid religious experiences of my life, are all in black and white. But when I remember her it is in color, and with scent."

I had yet to say a word. Honestly, I didn't know what to say. Actually, I wanted to scream and run.

"God seems anemic now," he smiled weakly. "But you know," still looking slightly off to the right, "I can close my eyes and actually feel my stomach shudder at the jiggle of her breasts. I can re-feel the unexpected jolt of thrill when she held my arms down and rode me."

If it had been Wilson telling me about a conquest I wouldn't have bat an eye; in fact I'd hoot and holler all along the way. But this guy was pathetic and disturbed. And even though I was as uncomfortable as if sitting on a crack, his sorrow poked me.

He slumped from his moment of sweet memory with a deep guttural sigh, and then a broken curvature of remorse returned him to the posture of confession. Awakened from his unfettered memory, he confided that he was haunted by guilty feelings that forever returned like a dog sniffing out a rabbit's scent. Guilt always bites any remnant of joy in the throat, he said

The intimacy of his erotic details was too personal for the steam room. I squirmed and felt myself search for a posture to indicate I was the Confessor listening but also in control of the room.

His life was a sequel to the Garden of Eden story, he confided, yammering more than confessing. The preacher never stopped talking and clearly I was an unnecessary element to his confession. He asked questions and answered them. He stared off into the distance and wandered around his past, then returned again to the present. I felt only slightly perturbed at my obvious irrelevance because, honestly, in my discomfort, I was also a titillated voyeur.

He agonized over the first time he met her and whether or not there was anything about that day that he could have done differently to prevent him from meeting her. The way he spun the story I could see why he's was a successful preacher. He told me his congregation was one of those massive suburban Wal-Mart style churches, a one-stop-shopping religious store with youth center, self-help groups for the recently divorced, grieved and lonely, a Mother's-Day-Out program, and whatever it takes to appeal to the consumer of faith.

I knew this guy. He was just like so many others in the "Helping Professions" who wear tiredness around the neck like a golden chain. The heaviness of their chosen burdens and self-affirmed purity of character cut deeply into their skin. They carry more than one world on their shoulders, and yet the burdens they heap upon themselves are at the bidding of a twisted ego.

Thankfully he dropped the self-torture stuff and slipped into a clear pool of memory.

In her presence, he said, he found himself full of something that had been absent for years. Even though he knew in advance there was an undertow of fatal attraction, he convinced himself his affection was *holy*. How could such feelings be bad when they fed him? She was a gift of water to a man struggling through the desert of mid-life and he was a gift to her. She told him so. It was so easy to rationalize those first visits, comforting him in the knowledge that meeting her was just for conversation, a small indulgence.

It started innocently enough, (exchanging phone numbers), but immediately they were talking every day. Talking on the phone became part of each other's daily routine. He called her at 8:30 every morning and then again when she got off work at 3:00 in the afternoon. They met for dessert and coffee or for walks where anyone who knew them would never stroll.

Even their first kiss could be rationalized, if never forgotten.

He was fifteen again, the preacher gushed. It was not a married kiss that had forgotten how to be surprised. Instead it began softly, with just the very tips of their lips scarcely touching. They hovered there, breathless, surging with blood then touching again. Firmer this time yet still restrained, exploring the taste and soft wet surface of one another's lips, fingers of lonely nerves feeling their way without sight. Then, unexpectedly, plunging with abandon; her tongue rivering his mouth first, deeply searching for more and more. She found his tongue and drew it through her lips with a breath and sucked on it. Chaos of sensations subsumed them in a tangle of touching that ended abruptly at the stick shift between them. Momentarily embarrassed they regained their postures and straightened themselves out before the inevitable jumble of excuses began to fall from their lips as demurely as their kiss was passionate.

That first kiss proved corrosive to the gate of his desires, he admitted as if it were a brand new insight. But she was a gift from God for a man who had to preach the love of the Almighty while receiving so little love himself.

What did his congregation expect when all they gave him was a little admiration? He drained himself week after week as he listened to their anxieties, stroked their grief and pacified their guilt, but who did that for him? Where was his confessor? Where was his counselor? Where was his guide through unfamiliar caverns? Surely this explosion of emotion wetting the landscape of his inner life and slaking his parched and tired spirit was a gift from above?

"You deserve to be loved," she would coo in his ear. "You deserve all good things," her soft young voice assured him. She loved him and he loved her. How could that be wrong? This was God rewarding a faithful servant who had sacrificed so much for so many.

Saying it out loud, he was embarrassed of course. He revealed the subterfuge now seemed astonishingly obvious and wondered how he had fooled himself so thoroughly. Why had he associated blood rushing to his capillaries and swelling his penis with God?

She stroked him with whatever words were needed to calm him. He knew now that she was not swimming in the water of true love, welcoming him into her body, even into her mouth, but not into her heart. How could she simply take him in without a grander vision or plan for the future? Unlike her, he had so many intricate scenarios populating his inflated fantasies that he had started to plan an escape from family and ministry.

"Surely God –" He stopped, paused, and looked at me. "If there is a God, will he not forgive the crass carnality of my body in favor of my purity of intention? Surely, if there is a God, that God would not have allowed a preacher to so easily trick himself into believing that pure sexual pleasure was sacred?"

At that moment Hamm pushed the door open. Like a child who waited too long to fulfill an impulse, he almost lunged toward the bench and flopped down between the preacher and me.

That ended it. The preacher stood up and left.

He did not look at me on the way out, confirming perhaps I was an inconsequential element of his confession. Maybe I was the witness to a conversation between mortal and divine, and sitting there to listen was all that the universe required. Even so there was a residual burden to my role: the preacher's query became mine. *Is there a God?*

I looked at Hamm, whose sprawl had seeped into the space where the preacher once sat. Gazing on the lump of human flesh before my eyes I thought to myself, *there can't be.*

Chapter Seven

When Why is not a Question

Estefan, with his perfectly white and perfectly shaped barbershop quartet mustache, pissed me off. It's not enough that he shaves in the steam room, he does it without shaving cream and the sound of a dry razor against whiskers grates on my nerves like fingernails on slate. He uses a blue plastic disposable safety razor and every time he intrudes upon the sanctuary of the steam room I am suddenly awash with images of hospitals I have known.

His happy little face fills my thoughts with invectives.

I was a nurse's aide once, a hapless college graduate unable to find a job and, looking back on it, an adolescent mind walking around in an adult body. On the first day of my first shift without two seconds of training, I met the depth of my fear and the shallowness of my soul.

Arriving as directed at seven in the morning, which was also the time when the outgoing nurses from the night shift met the incoming nurses from the day shift, they told me to walk around and see if anyone needed anything.

In my blue hospital uniform with a sparkling new photo-badge clipped on the pocket of my scrubs I felt oddly confident. All I needed was a stethoscope, I imagined, and I would look like a doctor. I walked the unfamiliar corridor passing by rooms and peeking in, trying to imagine what a patient might want that I could actually provide. I didn't have a clue where anything was located or what I could and couldn't do for anyone. Then it hit me, I had not been in a hospital since the day I was born. I knew nothing about them except what I had seen on television.

A disturbing sound grabbed my attention. It was a groan. I got closer and closer to it and soon could hear it as if a snoring partner next to me in bed. Emanating from the room at the corner of the hall, I looked in both directions for some assistance. There was no one there, not a movement or sound along either hallway. Practically tiptoeing up to the door I peeked around the frame as if to play peek-a-boo with a child. I saw the back of a man facing away from me as he sat on the edge of his bed. He was rocking forward then back again, groaning with each motion. Clearly in pain, the man was unaware I had entered the room.

"Can I help you?" I gulped.

He turned around, and when he did my face nearly fell off in shock at the deeply yellow color of his skin. I followed my instinct to run. Down the hall I fled in search of someone who could do something and to get as far away as possible from whatever turned him yellow. I knew nothing about jaundice and was flat out scared. It took several days before I even considered how that poor bastard felt as he sat on the bed suffering from whatever malady was taking whole bites out of his life only to have his condition reflected in my panic and fear.

Later that day, at the end of my first shift at the hospital, I was invited to attend the talent show put on by first year medical residents. It was a kind of hazing before the residents embarked upon the more elevated position of second year. I stumbled into the packed and overflowing auditorium to the incongruous sounds of raucous laughter and applause. On stage was a medical student representing the oncology unit dressed in hospital gown, bald wig, and fitted with a half filled urine bag on one side and an I.V. tote on the other. She was singing in an extraordinary voice for a doctor wannabe, to the tune of "You Light Up My Life." But the refrain of her re-worded ballad was, "You Prolong My Life". The audience of medical personnel and hospital employees were howling with laughter and catcalls. I was appalled.

Again, I left in horror and was completely shaken from being in the presence of caregivers laughing at the misery of those they treated. It took me about one week to understand the purpose and peculiar joy of such dark humor, and then I regretted having missed the rest of the show.

The other side of that hospital experience was an absolutely glorious several months of dating. A large urban hospital is full of young single women and men who want nothing more than to party away the rigors and emotional weight of the day. I never had a date with a resident or doctor but the dating buffet included nurses, technicians, social workers and even a chaplain.

All of that was why blue razors remind me of hospitals, and why hospitals occupy an exceptionally uneven terrain in my memory. The grim and somber memories still outweigh all the rest.

The first year I was an ordained minister, on the day before Christmas Eve, a truck hauling two semi-trailers jumped the meridian along an interstate and flipped. It landed on a minivan. The next day, on Christmas Eve, a nurse in my congregation called me to ask if I would visit the remnants of the unfortunate family who had travelled westward with no intention of stopping for death in our fair city.

One of the young teenage sons had been driving the family minivan. They were on their way to a grandparent's house for the Christmas holiday and giving the teenager some highway driving experience. The unfortunate driver was now in traction with multiple broken bones, cuts and abrasions. He would survive. His older brother, sitting behind him in the minivan, was dead upon arrival. The father, sitting next to him in the front, was alive but paralyzed from the neck down and likely never to move again. Only the mother, sitting behind the father, was almost completely unscathed.

In my days of wearing a collar and visiting the sick and shut-in, hospitals became as familiar as any other public space, but on my first morning as a nurse's aide every doorway into every patient room was a threshold of dread. On that day, that hospital room was darkened with only hallway light flooding its yellow hue onto pale dirty walls. The sundry machines with a spider web of tubes connected to them beeped and chimed intermittently, while green and red lights with white numerals glowed in the dark. I stepped quietly so as not to wake the boy who was crucified by chrome rods and wires on pulleys and stiffened with casts. The mother sitting in the corner behind me never made a sound and slipped my notice.

I stood at the boy's side, unsure of what to do, so I prayed quietly. It must have seemed a pathetically short and anemic prayer to the mother sitting there in the dark. "Is that all you got," she could have said with the smirking, trash-talking voice of an opponent on the basketball court.

It wasn't until I turned to leave that I saw her. She sat motionless, entombed in shadow.

The graceless arms that held her were from one of those ubiquitous hospital chairs of poorly stuffed vinyl. It was an avocado green chair, but don't ask me why I remember that. She wore a bright red sweater with some kind of holiday message stitched on it, something with a snowman and snowflakes. I stopped. For a long, slow moment I couldn't tell if she was breathing.

"Are you okay?" I asked stupidly.

"Why?" came a terse whisper.

"You were sitting there so quietly, I just wondered. Can I get you anything?"

"Why?" she asked again, low and breathier this time.

"I'm sorry, 'Why' what?" I asked with earnestness and utter incompetence.

"Why is my son dead and my husband ruined for the rest of his life, and Bobby all broken like this, and I don't even have a scratch? Why?"

I wanted to bolt just as I had from the yellow man. They don't teach answers to questions like that in seminary. The only thing I did right that day was to be speechless before her question. I just stood there. Actually, I think I froze there hearing everything with the acute awareness gushing adrenaline provides; the beeps and pulses and gurgles of the machines echoed around the barren room.

My thoughts stuttered on the question, turning it over and over and over again like a key in the ignition that can't fire a spark to turn over the engine. Then she spoke again.

"Why would God allow this to happen? We are churchgoers. We're Lutheran. Bob is the church treasurer and I am in the Martha Circle. My boys were both confirmed. What have we done to deserve this? Why?"

I don't remember what I said, nothing of consequence for certain. It wouldn't have been an offer to pray because that was a lightly used arrow in my quiver. Nor would I have tried to answer her question because I had no answers. Surely I said something. God, I hope I said something.

"Excuse me," was on my mind but I don't think I actually got it off my tongue before leaving the room.

That mother in the darkness has been with me for a long time now. She is still sitting there in my memory and asking me that question. Estefan's goddamn blue razor brings her back sometimes when I sit in the steam room where my mind and memory are free to wander.

There is no answer to that question.

Since then I have come to realize her question is a statement more than a question. It's not, "Why" as in, "Give me an answer." It is more, "Why have you done this to me!" It presupposes God's involvement because it is somehow more tolerable to imagine God acting despicably than it is to accept randomness. To accept nothing could have been done to avoid a massive truck landing flat upon your family's minivan, simply because you were in the wrong place at the wrong time, is more terrifying than believing that God is working his or her purpose out and that somehow, somewhere, there is method to the madness.

Some days I would sit in the steam room and remember that question, "Why?" It haunts me. Even though I now understand it is a statement more than a question, and even though I am more likely to choose randomness than providence when I allow it to infiltrate my thoughts, I find myself falling into a netherworld of troubling angels and demons. It is quicksand that has no bottom, and one in which the more I thrash the faster I sink.

Some days, when I fall in, Wilson or Frodo or Hamm save me. Other days I have to get up and leave the steam room before drowning in the bottomless questions.

Chapter Eight

On Second Chances

Occasionally, only in the depth of winter or on the wings of summer, a strange convergence renders the steam room an odd courtroom. It happens when the three ministers all land in it at the same time, and when I am there to hear.

I don't know them personally but they are well known at the The COE. A Presbyterian minister, a Roman Catholic priest, and the other a pastor from one of those splinter denominations Protestants have in abundance. It sounds like a joke: A Presbyterian minister, a Roman Catholic priest, and a Protestant pastor walk into a steam room. But it's true, they do.

It is rare for them to appear all at the same time, but when they do, and they hit the steam room together inevitably the conversation turns toward some bent rule or broken promise. As a failed holy man, I am reduced to the role of prosecutor or public defender before the tribunal.

Like the fallen tree in the forest, I suppose they could meet up all the time and I would never know. Isn't that just like a human being to presume if no one is there to hear it that it doesn't make a sound?

I opened the door and felt the outward rush of moist hot air against my dry body. They looked up and smiled but went on with their discussion. Four men in the Steam Room is a crowd but one of the corner seats was open so I sat down and made myself small. The moment I sat down the pipes banged and steam rose and I could study the three men without seeming lewd – two robed at the waist with towels and the third fully naked.

All three of them were on the smallish side, medium height or short. Two of them were slight and the third buff. I didn't actually know their names but in my steam room imagination I called them Darryl, Darryl, and Larry from the old Bob Newhart show. Larry is the shortest one. Darryl was telling a story.

"I get this call from the County Lock-up. It's the husband of one of my members."

"What's he in for," the other Darryl asked.

"Well ... child abuse," Darryl said bitterly, as if even saying it backwashed bile up his throat and left an acrid taste in his mouth.

"He was accused of sexually abusing his six year old daughter and three year old son. He'd been doing it for a couple of years and his wife came in and told me about it."

"What did you do when you heard about it," Larry asked with alarm.

"I convinced her to report it. But I had to

push her, you know, past her denial, you know, before she really could acknowledge it. It wasn't pleasant or easy, you know. You know what I mean, right?"

"Yes," Darryl and Larry assured him.

There was a momentary silence as Darryl appeared to be trying to decide how much of the story to tell and how to tell it. Then he sat up straight and leaned forward toward his two colleagues and showed utter disinterest toward my presence.

"But the judge released him, said he should get a second chance!" Darryl's eyes were as wide as saucers and his mouth hung open. Then, after a hefty pause, "He gives both him and the mother strict procedures and rules they have to follow, and sends the Dad off to counseling. Like that's going to help."

Darryl rolled his eyes and shifted positions a bit.

"So everything is quiet for about six months and then one day the mother comes home to find the six year old with her hands duct taped and the three year old with tape across his mouth and his hands tied."

"Oh my God," Larry exclaimed. "What was he going to do?"

"Well, no one is quite sure. The father had already fled, perhaps realizing what he was doing would land him in jail, and the kids gave confused and conflicting reports. All we really know is that by doing it he violated the court order and was picked up immediately and placed in jail where he is now awaiting sentencing."

"Wow, that was a near miss," Darryl breathed an audible sigh of relief.

"But didn't you say the father just called you from jail?" Larry asked.

"Yes, I just got off the phone with him before coming here. It was really disturbing. He was sobbing and sobbing. His wife told him she was filing for divorce and he begged me, begged me, to talk her out of it."

"You're kidding," Larry smirked.

"No, I'm not, he sounded absolutely desperate. 'Please, p-l-e-a-s-e' he sobbed and pleaded, 'Don't I deserve a second chance?' You should have heard him – it was so pathetic. I couldn't help but feel sorry for him. 'Help me please, you have to help me' he sobbed, and just kept repeating it, 'Doesn't everyone deserve a second chance?' Well, what was I supposed to say?"

There was silence in the steam room.

The pipes stopped clanging as the steam reached a crescendo and the zenith of its slow disappearing act. The other Darryl and Larry seemed to be waiting, not anxious to weigh in on the question.

"I never felt compassionate toward a pedophile before," Darryl confessed, finally breaking the silence. "I mean, when the whole drama was unfolding it seemed pretty black and white – the guy's an asshole and needs to be eliminated from the family. It was a real absolute, clear-cut situation, right?"

"Yeah, seems pretty absolute," Larry confirmed.

"Right," the other Darryl said.

"Yeah, that's how I felt too," Darryl continued. "But if you could have heard the sobbing, you would have been moved. He was so desperate and so alone and I was the only one he knew to reach out to. I started feeling sorry for the guy."

"But you didn't promise him anything did you?" Larry asked nervously, as if suddenly he wasn't confident in how Darryl handled the situation.

"No, I'm just saying it was hard. On the other end of that phone, wailing and suffering like he was, he wasn't just a pedophile any more. He was more than that – he was a man who needed help and was facing a horrendous future."

"Well, yeah, I can see that ..." the other Darryl said hesitantly.

"What did you tell him," Larry quipped impatiently.

"I told him he had his second chance. I told him the judge gave him his second chance and that he blew it. I told him that his wife was exactly right to divorce him because the children were the most vulnerable ones in the situation and they need to be protected."

"What did he say to that," Darryl wanted to know.

"He wailed and begged again. Then he played the Christian Card. 'But Christians have to forgive. We have to forgive! Don't I deserve to be forgiven too?' he pleaded."

"Yes, I told him. Christians are asked to forgive but that doesn't mean forget, and it doesn't mean allowing violence and betrayal to go on without intervention. You may have another chance someday, I told him, but it won't be with your wife and it won't be with your children – at least not while they are young and vulnerable. You may have another chance with someone else and I hope you find a way to make it work. That's what I said."

"He's toast," Larry said.

"Yeah, he won't make it out of prison, do you think?" Darryl mused.

"Who knows?" the other Darryl said dismissively.

After another period of silence, Darryl looked up at the other two and asked, "Do you think I said the right thing?"

"I think you were amazingly compassionate, considering," Larry said flatly.

"Just right," said Darryl.

"What a weird job we have," Larry added, just a little throwaway line.

"Yeah, sometimes it's pretty weird," both Darryls agreed.

The three ministers looked over at me and I smiled, maybe even gave a little involuntary shrug. Darryl got up and declared he had a couple to meet with for premarital counseling. Larry said he had a finance meeting to attend and the other Darryl said his Justice Commission was meeting and he had to be there. All three left together, each one offered a polite smile on the way out.

I wondered about compassion for a pedophile.

What would it be like to get that phone call from jail? Most people probably don't think about ministers doing stuff like that, I knew such a scenario would be the farthest thing from my mother's mind. She thought all I did was to parade around in robes, scold people from the pulpit, hold forth at funerals and weddings, and ask for money. How could I have screwed up such a cake job, she always asked in front of her friends, and then they would laugh.

The image of those three ministers sitting there with elbows leaning in on their thighs, heads bent and looking down into the well of wonderment while trying to decide about the right thing to do, even for a pedophile, brought a flush of affection. How much crueler the world would be without them, without the small legion of oddballs doing that peculiar work and holding so much pain?

"I did that once," I said to the empty room, then stretched out in a full prone position just like Hamm would do while the steam did its magic.

Chapter Nine

Hamm's Dilemma

"Let me ask you a question," Hamm snarled.

It came as a surprise because we shared the steam room for the better part of five years and that many words had never flowed between us at any one time in all those years. My sense of dread in anticipation of the next question was only exceeded by the shock of its intimacy.

"Shoot."

"Do you love your wife?"

Is that a trick question? The moat rolled out, the bars slammed shut, the appearance of my castle guards was immediate. That was dangerous ground between men, especially relative strangers. Men don't speak casually about the delectable layers life has to offer. Hamm's question was like asking, "When did you stop beating your wife," except it was tinged with the urgency and sweat of real life. And it was *Hamm*, whom I didn't like or trust.

"I'm not married," I said, "but we've lived together for twelve years – I figure that's as good as married."

"But you love her, right?"

Then I got it. He didn't want to know

whether I really loved her or not, he was assuming I did. Whoa, I had almost ventured where I didn't need to go!

"Right," I said, hoping the relief in my voice didn't register.

"So, let me ask you something."

Hamm's whole body flopped in the open, the way a dog rolls on its back with legs spread in utter unselfconscious repose. I didn't assume other men wanted to see all of me while Hamm never drew the curtains. More to the point, I ask myself how the people around me might feel in a given situation and Hamm had probably never thought to ask that question in his life. It seemed pretty clear he had never given a thought about how the rest of us felt in the presence of his dog-flop.

"You like the way she looks?"

I suddenly realized that even though I had sat naked with this guy for five years, I had no more idea whether Hamm was kidding or serious than I did about what the Russian Ambassador ate for breakfast. Frozen inside, the silence thundering in my ears, I felt as blank as my stare.

"I mean, does she still look good to you?" he asked more urgently, as if rephrasing it this way was going to make the question palatable.

"Well ..." I stammered a bit to buy time. "I guess it depends on my mood. There isn't much mystery any more if that's what you mean."

"No man, I'm talking about what she fucking looks like," he growled.

"Yeah, she still looks good to me, if my only choice is 'yes' or 'no'."

"Well let me ask you something else then," he said as if he hadn't asked enough. "What if she was fat?"

"How fat?"

"Pretty fat."

"Well, like how fat?"

"Like a fucking donut, man. I mean like, fat, in all the places: between her legs, under her arms, a little bit around the neck, droopy in the butt and the ankles. I hate it when the ankles are fat."

Being a visual person I had no trouble conjuring the image he had drawn but it wasn't anyone in particular. I see the body parts in the film room behind my closed eye: lumps and folds of skin, the odd textures of rippled and dimpled fat, the motion of bulbous flesh as it jiggles.

"Well ..." Hamm asked as if I knew what he meant.

"Well what?"

"Well, would you?"

"Would I what?"

"Would you want to fuck her, man? Would you want to have her?"

What the hell? What is this maniac asking me? I heard my thoughts shouting.

I abruptly realized I didn't even know his real name. Hamm was one of my made-up names. I was tempted to ask his name just to poke at the incredible assault on decorum his questions had marshaled. He asked me to tell him something more personal than I would tell my own partner, maybe even my therapist. *Who is this guy*? I thundered inside my head.

"Dude, why you asking me?" I demanded.

Now *his* silence filled the steam room. Good, the discomfort was where it belonged.

"Well ... because, man, I can't stand to look at my wife anymore and I want to know if that's natural."

Whoa, hold on. The traffic in my head screeched to a standstill.

Hamm, after all these years of silent distance in which we simply occupied the same space at the same time, with me harboring an ill will that may or may not be shared, was forcing the lock and trying to enter into intimacy with me?

But men are like that.

We go along traveling together in silent distances and suddenly with as little warning as a cloudburst, the distance is penetrated by a single intimacy. Then, after the need has been resolved, the distance returns and might never be breached again.

"What am I going to do, man?" he whimpered softly.

At once Hamm was drenched in humanity. His lament pulled an instinctive cord of empathy I was unable to resist.

Even though Hamm had not moved an inch, his dog flop collapsed into a heap. In an instant his five-year aggressive demeanor was revealed to be a thin and sorrowful shell dissolving all around him. This suddenly humanized form painfully poked at the embers of compassion burning in the hollow of my gut, but still I could find no words to say.

"Did you ask her to lose weight?" I knew it was lame the minute I asked it.

"Yeah, man, we've talked about it. I even told her I'd go to weight-watchers with her – you know the whole weigh-in deal and count calories. I said I'd do it. She just keeps eating like there's no tomorrow."

"Does she exercise?" Still lame, but I was buying time.

"Yeah, you probably seen her upstairs. She does the elliptical and the treadmill and takes a step class too. But it's the eating, man, it's the eating. Exercise can't make up for feeding at the trough."

I am afraid of the question, like Lot's wife who can't resist turning around to watch the destruction of Sodom and Gomorrah even though she knew it would be fatal if she did. But I asked, tip-toeing gingerly as I did.

"Did you tell her you're not attracted to her anymore?"

"Yeah man, it was awful. But it's been a long time coming. It's been years. I'm not expecting Marilyn Monroe or anything but something, you know? I mean, come on."

"So how fat is she, really? I mean, on a scale from 1 to 10?"

"Seriously? She's a seven, man, working toward an eight."

"What would be acceptable to you?"

"I could live with a five or six, you know? A five or six would be good."

"Okay, here's the question. Can you have sex without being attracted to her physically? I mean, you still love her, right?"

"Well, yeah, I still love her, but after a while it's all mixed up in there, isn't it? I mean, how you gonna separate the physical and everything else?"

Boy, if I had the answer to that I would be the Guru of Love and replace Phil and Dear Annie.

They say women can fall in love with a face, a personality, even a voice sometimes, but with men it's the body or even one part of it. She can have the greatest personality and even a sexy voice, but if the body has come off its wheels the wagon of romance gets stuck in the mud.

"Mind over matter, my friend," I said with the confidence of a con artist. "Love is of the mind, not the body. You've got to let your mind do the work and hold her in the arms of your mind while you've got her body posting on your saddle horn. You know?"

"Mind over matter," he repeated it to himself like memorizing a phone number. "Mind over matter."

I listened to him mutter as thoughts of love and sex raced through my mind. Hamm drifted into silence and the steam pipes clanged, announcing a new dawn of vapor.

When I was young and dating for the fun of it I adopted a rationalist perspective that sex between humans was no different than sex between cows and bulls, except that we accorded our species a higher status and genital sex the sacrament of love. Then, when I got married and began having children I was able to adorn the same act of physicality with mystery, even a mystical quality that was not there before. Now, divorced and re-partnered, I can read in the act of intercourse something more than science but much less than religion.

A rabbi once pointed out to me something unique about Jesus I never learned in seminary.

When the Scribes queried Jesus about divorce, the rabbi said, they wanted to know which of the great rabbis Jesus agreed with, Hillel or Shammai? It turns out they both allowed divorce because it was codified in the ancient law in the Book of Deuteronomy. But like the Supreme Court interpreting the Constitution, these two giants of Jewish history disagreed about the acceptable grounds for divorce. What did Jesus think was an acceptable condition for divorce, the Scribes wanted to know.

My rabbi friend pointed out that Jesus

did not base his opinion upon the sacred text in Deuteronomy as Hillel and Shammai did. Jesus leafed further back in the Bible to a story in the book of Genesis in which it says a man and a woman are made one flesh and therefore, because God put them together, they can never be rent apart. Is that true? Would Jesus now think that was also true for same sex marriages too?

Looking over at Hamm who was clearly pacing the floor in the basement of his soul, I thought about my ex-wife and my current partner, and their faces set off multiple explosions of pain.

Divorce is not separation, I suddenly realized as if a meteor striking earth, it's an amputation. Jesus was right. Once we have connected, flesh-to-flesh, we are connected whether we like it or not, even when we separate. Like they told my kids in their high school sex education classes, we don't just have sex with the person to whom we are genitally attached in the moment, we have sex with all the people *they* ever had sex with, too. That is a "degree of separation" no one wants to think about.

"You know, after all these years, I really do love her. She's not how I want her to be, but I still love her." Hamm looked genuinely stunned at the realization.

"Well, Hamm, you're probably not exactly how she wants you to be either, I can guarantee you that!" I smirked.

He chuckled then said, "My name's not Hamm. Where'd you get that?"

"Oh, uh, I dunno."

"Name's Lucian. What's yours?"

"Craig. But everyone calls me Spin."

I like the name Hamm a lot better. He'd never know that I kept calling him that in my head, but after that I always called him Lucian in the steam room.

The door opened and Wilson squeezed in. That massive oval shape topped with the doo-rag all wrapped in a shiny sweat suit evoked a smile and the warm feeling of family. But Hamm jumped up and out of his spread-eagle lounge in a Pavlovian reflex amazing to behold. He was gone in an instant. But when I chuckled along with Wilson over Hamm's retreat, it was with affection instead of spite.

Chapter Ten

Superman's Ballad

"Hey there Delilah ..." Roger sang.

I plopped down on the bench outside the steam room that faced the entrance to the shower chamber and paused to figure out what to do.

Roger sings in the steam room.

He sits in there for up to an hour with his first-generation iPod Shuffle wrapped in a plastic baggie and performs woeful medleys of pop tunes. On the day in question, I sat morose, head in hands, outside the steam room listening to him wail away on the second and third verses of the Plain White T's ballad.

Roger could be a character in a Saturday Night Live skit. Wearing a huge cobalt blue boxer swimsuit tied around his chest just south of the nipples, the trunks still nearly touched his kneecaps. A hair swivel rested atop his head; a long strand of hair rooted like a flag to the hole on a golf green that curled around in a labyrinth to cover as much hairless surface as possible. This combination of oddities was caricature enough to cause Roger to stand out in any crowd but add to it the Elton John glasses with a slight blue tint, and he truly was one of a kind. He wore those glasses in the steam room where they fogged beyond color, and he wore them in the shower with suds dripping down the pane. It wouldn't surprise me if Roger's glasses eventually became affixed to the flesh behind his ears the way a tree can envelope an alien object over time.

The chorus of, "Hey there, Delilah," trailed off and I felt a jolt of hope, a tingling thrill that the concert was over. I had been sitting there on the bench the entire time Roger was serenading Delilah, and because it is one of those grilled wooden benches with half an inch between each slat, my butt was a burger in need of flipping.

Ugh, my hopefulness was quashed as he began singing again – "I can't stand to fly, I'm not that naïve ..."

Shit.

My girlfriend hates "Superman (It's Not Easy)" by Five for Fighting but I like it, at least when Roger is not singing it. I've decided it is about men and how we are taught not to cry, and how that fucks us up until we can learn to cry again.

Once, when I first left the Catholic priesthood and struggled with what to do next, I went to group therapy. The therapist asked us to prepare a song for the next session, one we would sing to the group. I think I heard my sphincter muscle pop.

It takes a lot of balls to sing in front of

anybody but imagine a therapy group in which each person is going to be asked what the song reveals about him or her. When we started the session the very first guy to stand up was a diminutive, quiet man who almost never said a word. He was one of those guys who always dresses the same: loafers without socks, chino's pressed at the dry cleaners, a natty little golf shirt with the collar turned up, horn-rimmed glasses and very dark black hair parted like the Red Sea and never out of place. Bravely and without a word, he walked to the center of the circle with arms flat against his sides as if scaffolding that held him up. Then he made a little gurgling noise to clear his throat. The next thing out of his mouth was, "I can't stand to fly, I'm not that naïve."

When he finished he turned without a word, kept his eyes cast downward toward his shoes while walking back to the chair, and sat down. Raindrops were streaming down the flats of my cheeks and when I finally looked up, I could see there wasn't a dry eye around the circle except for the guy who sang who was still looking down at the floor.

We talked about all the ways men are taught not to cry, how we were made to feel ashamed if we showed fear, and who we learned to hide our feelings from.

It was as if we were all raised in the same household, each one instructed by the whip of humiliation. Before that group experience I had imagined it was just in my house and in my neighborhood, but that night all of us were reminiscing about total strangers who went out of their way to say humiliating things to us as boys, sternly reminding us not to show too much emotion.

As I listened to Roger sing the part in which Superman complains he is not allowed to cry, I imagine in my mind the guy standing there singing to all of us so many years before

But I also felt incredulous. Sitting there outside the steam room, Roger's voice sounding like Pluto howling a song to Mickey Mouse, I could still feel the pressure of tears gathered behind my eyes in what I call the Wolfman Syndrome. It's when a man tries to hold back tears, the irrefutable feeling of warmth spreading out across his face, collecting in the sinuses underneath the upper cheekbones and pushing its way up until it stings the eyeballs. As all that is happening, he knows it is a losing battle and he had better get someplace where no one will see the final transformation take place. No one wants to see a grown man cry.

The stinging in my eyes pushed forward memories from across decades and miles, from all the way back in sixth grade. My teacher, Mr. Piazza was a short tight man who wore a grim expression on the mask of his face. He did not like Saul Podick or me, both of us six feet tall by the middle of our sixth grade year, and thus several inches taller than

Mr. Piazza.

During "Work Alone Time" when we were supposed to be reading or writing, if he caught us leaning back in our chairs he would sneak up from behind and yank us by the collar onto the floor. He only did that to Saul and me. If he thought we weren't paying attention when he talked in front of the class, he would throw the long white foam eraser at us with deadly accuracy. He only did that to Saul and me.

Saul was wicked smart but not particularly clever, and would keep M&M's in his shirt pocket so that he could sneak them one by one into his mouth. Mr. Piazza would catch him of course, then order Saul to take them out of his pocket and place them palm up in his hand. Mr. Piazza would then slap Saul's hand and watch them fall to the floor where he would step on them one by one before making Saul clean them up.

I was a very slow reader, which was an endless source of pain and embarrassment. We had a reading system in those days in which different paced readers used color-coded booklets. The fastest readers were in the purple section long before the rest of us, and as most of my friends were "Purple Readers" it was all the more hurtful that I lagged several colors behind. Mr. Piazza relished having me read out loud and smiled silently as I stammered and stumbled over words.

One day, after being screamed at by Mr. Piazza for what is now a long forgotten offense or act of stupidity, he marshaled me out of the room with the door slamming against my ass. I walked slowly along the long marble tiled corridor to the Assistant Principal's office with my chin sagging to my chest and the back of my hand feeling the cool of the concrete wall. That old familiar feeling of tears rushed into the reservoir behind my eyes and howled danger. Just then a hand reached into mine and held it, still walking.

That hand belonged to Mr. Audable, the other sixth grade teacher. My best friend was in Mr. Audable's class and it made me jealous because Audable was kind and caring in all the ways adolescent boys often miss.

"You're just fine," he said. "I'll talk to Dr. Forrester for you."

We walked to Dr. Forrester's office together, hand in hand, without my feeling the least embarrassed about it. I could hear mumbling inside Dr. Forrester's office and then Mr. Audable came out and told me I could go back to class.

"And remember, you're just fine," he assured me.

Before that day, stuck outside the steam room listening to Roger sing, I hadn't thought about that event in decades. Roger's coyote voice managed to carry me a long, long way back. What would happen if he could actually sing?

But he couldn't and just as I was softened ever so slightly to Roger's occupation of the steam room he started singing, "Flashdance ... What a Feeling."

Fantasies of Jennifer Beals aside, Roger's howling sucked all warmth and tenderness out of me like a toilet plunger; all except the unfortunate image of him trying to dance like Beals in the confines of the steam room. At that I chuckled. There was nothing to do but shower and go home.

Chapter Eleven

Maggie Mae

"Hey, Surfer Dude!"

She called me that because on 'the outside' I wore the same thing almost every day: a Hawaiian shirt and baggy cargo pants. Even in Buffalo's frigid winter I was as likely to wear sandals as boots.

Her name was Mary and she sat at the front desk of The COE and assigned a different handle to every member – or at least those friendly enough to evoke one.

I called her Maggie, a la Rod Stewart, and because she looked like a Maggie Mae I knew once.

"It's too damn early, Maggie. I don't want to do this shit." I felt slight remorse for growling in the face of her sunshine.

"It's good for you, Surfer Dude!" she said with a smile that was way too earnest and sweet for 6:30 AM. Almost everything Maggie said had an exclamation or question mark at the end of it.

"I don't see you exercising, Miss Maggie Mae," I snarked over my shoulder, descending the stairs to the locker room with the fragile gait of a man twice my age.

"Don't need to, Surfer Dude, I look this good without it!"

Maggie weighed more than me by a good twenty pounds but carried herself as if she was a Rock Star in hot pants and bra. I love people who are fat, butt ugly or deeply flawed in some obvious way and who don't seem to give a shit. I marvel at them. At the same time it causes the dark angel in my brain to look for tell-tale cracks revealing all is not well inside them. I slip into their eyes in search of even a wisp of self-hatred, and if I find it, that little angel does a goal line celebration dance.

I am not proud of it, but I can't get rid of it either.

Once the sour taste of self-consciousness backs up in my throat about how flabby, old and broken down I feel, a dark figure lurking inside will say nasty things about a sweetheart like Maggie. This shrunken ghoul inside is a nasty little hairless flesh-eating creature. He stands in the shadow and smirks, calling out warnings that nice people are passive-aggressive, and no one is truly nice. Sometimes the things he says are cruel beyond belief, but funny. So funny it makes the good angel who flits around in the brighter side of my brain burp out a laugh without meaning to, and then has to stuff it down again.

Last year Maggie's mom died and she moved through the grief and pain of death as gracefully as a dragonfly flits from one delicate perch to the next, alighting on each ache and taking off again with the appearance of effortlessness. She had the kind of a simple faith that neither questions how nor why, which incites my dark angel.

Listen to that idiot, he'd whisper in my ear as Maggie told me about what God had done for her that day, even though her day would offer any normal sourpuss a smorgasbord of complaints. She's too stupid to know if she's on fire, he would whisper while I was listening outwardly with as much earnestness on my face as I saw on hers.

Maggie told me in detail about her mother dying. She said her mom had tried everything known to animal and man to cure her cancer. Once she was diagnosed she started out with chemotherapy, but the chemical cocktails had no impact and the doctor gave her no hope for remission. She drove to the Cleveland Clinic for another opinion, but they concurred with the local physician. Then her mom tried the Mayo Clinic with the same result. Then, being a woman of means, she found a hospital in NYC that was conducting an experimental trial with other desperate patients. That proved ineffective as well. Someone told her about a shaman, or witchdoctor, or something even more bizarre in a remote village in Mexico and she made Maggie take her down there. No one can say whether it would have happened anyway but she came back from the witchdoctor in remission.

Home again and leaving nothing to chance, Maggie escorted her mom on round after round of visits to Buffalo's finest healers, acupuncturists and yogis. I was astounded to hear there were so many practitioners of alternative medicine and hocus-pocus right here in Western New York. Maggie added up the total cost of those efforts once, but wouldn't tell me how much it was. All she would say is it was less, even with the trip to Mexico, than what the insurance company paid the hospital for her tests and chemotherapy. In the end, her mom lasted about sixteen months from the initial diagnosis, which was within the margin of death her first doctor offered.

Maggie's mom went to hospice about two weeks before dying and she dragged me there to visit her. In my holy man days the hospice was one of my favorite places to visit. In nursing homes, even the dressed up ones where rich people think it will be better at the end, the smell of urine and echoes of moaning is depressing. But that is not what hospice is like.

I didn't know her mom from Adam but Maggie's twisted demeanor of sweet and pathetic hooked my guilt and I couldn't say no.

Maggie said her mom loved male visitors and asked me please, please, would I go for a visit. Flowers in hand, I went with her to the suburban village of buildings nestled under a canopy of shade trees. It was on the cusp of summer when spring flowers and new greens are most vibrant, and as we turned into the parking lot I remember the sensation of seeing the hospice cottages framed by the colors and fragrances of life at its most scintillating.

I don't recall how many rooms there are to a cottage, but because they were single story buildings with Cape Cod cedar shingles, it gave the impression of intimacy and charm. Immediately inside visitors were greeted by a massive fish tank large enough for a five year old to swim a lap or two. The lighting and textures were purely domestic with an ambiance nothing like a hospital or nursing home.

When we entered the room, Maggie's mom was sitting up in bed reading a book. The room was large, big enough to be a parlor, with a giant window on the wall opposite the door. Dark wood furniture in abundance, more than necessary for the task, was scattered about the room and the bed a matching four-poster without canopy. The big flat television stood dark and silent. Instead, music from an mp3 dock was audible. Classical music lilted in the background the same way a subtle but sweet fragrance owns a room. She set down her book and smiled.

"Is this your new young man," she sparkled.

Maggie blushed as I looked at her with surprise.

"I'm not that young, ma'm," I retorted.

"No, mom, this is my friend," she began to say but was cut off by a loud sneeze emanating from her mother.

"Bless you!" I beat Maggie to it.

"No, I am a friend from The Cohen Center, but I would like to know more about the mysterious new boyfriend." Then I turned to Maggie who still blushed.

Maggie cleared her throat and asked her mom how she felt, then immediately began straightening up and busying around what was an otherwise peaceful scene. I sat down and watched Maggie's anxiety act itself out, and observed her mother's benign amusement at her daughter's obvious love and worry.

"Sit down," her mom finally ordered.

Maggie sat down on the chair nearest the bed then motioned for me to pull my chair over close to hers rather than against the wall at the end of the bed where I watched from a distance.

"I am dying, you know," she said flatly while looking me straight in the eyes. I couldn't tell if she was searching for a reaction, measuring my mettle, or simply stating the obvious in order to clear the air.

I liked her immediately.

"What's that like?" I asked nonchalantly though inside I felt like tiptoeing out the door.

"Well, right now I am angry," she said

with the vim and vigor of a woman who was used to directing whatever scene she was in.

"Mother, what are you angry about? Have they been neglecting you? Because we can –"

"No! They are fine. They are more than fine in fact. The nurses are perfect, and the aids are polite, and one of them is quite cute, and if I am going to need any physical assistance I will call for him."

We both chuckled, though her mom wore a straight face that was all business.

"No, I am angry that I am still *here*."

"But mother, I want you to be here as long as you can be. I need you."

This was the first splash of tears and anguish I heard seep out of Maggie, and the angel of my darker nature smiled and wagged his head in a knowing kind of way, as if to say, I told you so.

"Well, you can't keep me, dear. I am dying, and as far as I am concerned I should have gone by now."

"Why do you say such things, mother?" Maggie looked at the floor rather than her mother's eyes.

"Look," she said, starring directly at Maggie, "everyone who I love has been here. I have said good-bye to my life-long friends – Gwyneth called from Portland, did I tell you?"

Maggie smiled and shook her head.

"The grandchildren have been here more than once, and it is very hard on them. You and your sister have been here and we have talked and decided upon which one of you will take what furniture and jewelry. We have made our amends for old wounds and spoken tenderly. I have said good-bye to the world and I have told God I am ready. The priest has been here, for Christ's sake. I went to sleep last night expecting to die and I woke up this morning angry. That's why!"

Maggie was quiet and I wasn't about to speak up.

"Mother," she said softly after a minute, "you're not in charge."

"Well of course I am not in charge! That is precisely what bothers me. If I were God, and a person had tidied things up the way I have, I would have better timing than He seems to."

"Mother!" Maggie scolded. "That is no way to talk."

"Oh for crying out loud, Maggie, God can handle my nits and nats. You think I will stop being me in heaven? You think that when you get there and we see each other again I am going to be mellower than my earthly self? Hah! You'll be surprised. Your father and I are going to take up right where we left off before he died so suddenly, because I was winning an argument when he so rudely passed. Right now that is what I am looking forward to most."

I was able to laugh given my emotional distance from the characters involved and

Maggie's mom seemed to appreciate that I could hear the humor in her speech even if Maggie could not.

That hospice scene flooded my thoughts as I ambled slowly down the stairs to the locker room with Maggie's retort still hanging in the air behind me. The atmosphere and moment of that hospice room stayed with me on the elliptical machine and Stairmaster, and kept hanging around while I strengthened my legs on the Cybex machines. Somewhere between stretching on the thick blue exercise mat with Stevie Nicks singing "Landslide" in my ear and sitting down in front of my locker, I briefly forgot about it.

I got caught up in watching Dweedle sitting at the end of the bench reading the newspaper.

"Any good news today?" It's that dark angel priming the pump.

"They're no fuckin' good. The bastards are no fuckin' good," he said without looking up to determine who asked.

"Hey, can I ask you a personal question?" I ventured.

Dweedle's head pivoted on his shoulders like an owl. His chest faced away from me but his oversized shiny bald forehead, droopy eyes, and goofy grin looked back at me.

"When you had your heart attack, did you think you were going to die?"

"Never thought about it," he grunted.

"Never?"

"Nope, I was too uncomfortable to think about it. Besides, I knew most of those bastards from the Fire Department and EMT running around and I was more worried about them screwing up than I was thinking about dying from whatever was going on inside my chest."

"Yeah, but once you found out what had happened, did you think about dying?"

"What the fuck? What's the point of thinking about dying? You wanna know if I'm scared? No, I'm not scared of dying. My day will come and I hope it is as far away as possible, but when it comes it comes. That's all."

"You're Jewish, right?"

"Yeah."

"Do Jews believe in life after death?"

"Jews believe in whatever the fuck they wanna believe in. I don't believe in life after death. This is it, kid, you better get used to the idea. It's now or never."

"You mean, when you die that's all there is? Nothing afterward, just, you know, dirt?"

"Just dirt, kid."

Dweedle turned around and buried his face in the newspaper. I lost my clothes in a pile in front of locker 88, my locker, and wrapped my purple towel like a skirt. I closed the padlock, spun the dial and headed for the steam room deep in thought.

"That Dennis, he's a corker," Dweedle muttered as I passed.

The Steam Room Diaries

I was alone in the steam room. Ah! But ugh, without the steam that room was so white and light and barren I could hardly stand it. I grabbed the hose and sprayed the thermostat as if putting out a fire. A cloud of steam and the sting of heat wrapped me in a cocoon.

In younger days, when I was married and our children were small, we had a neighbor whose two-year old daughter developed Leukemia. It was heart-wrenching and even now I squirm to think about it. The little girl, Jenny, was a two-year-old with spectacular charm, a veritable morsel of yumminess. Her parents were less than that, even in the best of times. The mother knew no boundaries on her way to arranging her family's life and that of the entire neighborhood, and always around her particular needs and desires. The father was a mush of passivity and seething anger, rolled out by subjugation to his wife and flattened by depression.

When Jenny began to bruise without cause the normal medical protocols were followed. To the horror of everyone who knew her, she was declined for any further treatment at local hospitals because she was deemed a poor candidate for success. No one could have had more visits in the Children's Hospital than that little girl, as one by one the neighborhood and other friends came by with stuffed animals, food, flowers, balloons, books and games. We despaired with Jenny's parents as she became more lethargic and pale in her hospital crib with bars made in the shape of zoo animals.

Then word came that Jenny had been accepted into an experimental bone-marrow transplant program at a Children's Hospital in Missouri. We packed up Mom and Jenny and sent them off while Dad stayed home trying to manage their other children who had already learned from their mother how to run roughshod over him. The neighbors pitched in with food and transportation and, behind his back, we shook our heads at his incompetence as a parent.

Mother and daughter returned home weeks later to wait for test results that would determine if the experimental treatment worked. The waif of a child seemed even smaller now and, we were told, it had been an excruciating procedure. All that was left was to hope against hope. Each family in the neighborhood said prayers every night for Jenny and her family, and so the awareness of life's fragility and the proximity of death's rancid breath came early to the children along our street. Finally the test results returned and the mood was grim.

The next thing we heard Jenny's mother had applied to every experimental program she could find, at every cancer institute and children's hospital across the country. Before the end came she had chased a cure at seven hospitals, each effort as invasive and painful as the previous one. Jenny simply shrank into oblivion from the torture of bone and blood exchanges, none of which had any positive impact on the child.

The mother would not give up no matter what the cost to her diminishing daughter, as she traded any possible quality of life for false hope. All of us understood the anguish of Jenny's parents but none of us could excuse the extent to which this woman sought to bend the iron certainty of death with her bare hands at the expense of her daughter's suffering.

At Jenny's funeral there was at least as much anger present toward the mother and nebbish of a father as there was sorrow and grief. Even so many years later, rubbing my face to get the image of Jenny out of my thoughts, I felt anger as the door opened and Wilson ambled in.

I grunted a salute and Wilson grunted one back as he poured a dribble of his elixir on the pipes. Up rushed the pungent aroma like walking into a beer freezer on a hot day. I tried to flush the images and memories of death from behind my eyes but they circled the drain and stubbornly resisted my push.

Then a daydream filled my skull and in it I saw Maggie's mom, Dweedle, and both of Jenny's parents pulling a thick, braided tug-of-war rope, and on the other end was the diminished Jenny pulling back all by herself. Jenny did not exert much effort but stood her ground; rope wrapped around her waist and heels dug into grassy soil. The adults at the other end of the rope were huffing, puffing and grunting in an effort to defeat the little girl but still she resisted them.

It is a strange image, I know, but there it was at the base of my brain like a wad of hair in the sink. I wondered what it meant. Mercifully Wilson was silent that day leaving me space to wonder.

Chapter Twelve

The Stripper

It was a Wednesday and neither Wilson nor Hamm were anywhere to be seen. With Wilson that usually meant he was on some hip-hop adventure out of town but I knew very little about the mysteries of Hamm's existence.

Otherwise it had been a pretty routine morning, nothing special at all; a modest workout, profuse sweating, a parade of aging naked bodies trudging through their post-breakfast, pre-work routines. The men's locker room was like the train station with personal schedules that for most of us had been ground and polished to a fine precision by years of repetition: 8 o'clock would find Estefan shaving in front of a sink if he didn't shave in the steam room, a tidy white terry towel wrapped around his tidy waist; 8:05 Frodo arrived at the sink alongside Estefan, butt-naked and ready to shave; by 8:20 Frodo was dressed to a predictably natty finish and brushing his teeth as the pièce de résistance. So it was a little strange when that morning Estefan had already left the locker room by the time Frodo finished up; both of them gone. Dweedle read on the bench and Ted, whom you have not met yet, was on the john reading the paper waiting for the snail in his bowels to crawl out.

I wallowed in splendid isolation, grinning ear-to-ear from my blessed solitude in the steam room. Occasionally I opened one eye to peek through the sweaty glass just to make sure the world beyond still ticked by in an orderly fashion and nothing was out of place. My skin was as glossy as a rotisserie chicken. Boiled water dripped off the ceiling and landing randomly on my exposed skin.

Jackson!

He gave a grand salute on the way in and I saluted back, mine not quite as crisp. He plopped down in the corner, feet on the floor, back leaning against the white tile of the walls where they came together.

Jackson is one of Buffalo's Finest, a cop with nearly thirty years, and considering retirement at the tender age of fifty-eight. Buffalo cops have a legalized scam whereby their pension is based on the last two years of income, so they work like dogs for twenty-four months, jacking up their pensions with copious amounts of over-time. There was a front page story in *The Buffalo News* about one old cop who retired with a pension that paid him over a hundred and fifty grand or about twice what he made for the first twenty-eight years. I admit to some jealousy over their pensions, but I have never envied them the danger, drudgery or nastiness of a job that benefits the rest of us.

Whatever his pension, I like Jackson. He was one of those guys who offered to get what you need, to solve whatever problem you had, especially trouble-shooting any issue you might have with the city or its courts. He even helped expedite the filing of my divorce papers, impressing my attorney with the reach of his influence.

Jackson was in mid-sentence, talking about a judge neither one of us liked, when the door opened and a tall, slender woman in a bikini walked in and sat down like there was nothing strange about it. I didn't know why but my first instinct was to run.

All those seventh grade emotions flushed through my veins as if someone just caught me smoking behind the school. I resisted the temptation to bolt and instead, eased my back up against the wall slowly so as to appear nonchalant. I felt myself flatten my belly without instruction. *Thank God I'm wearing a towel today*, the voice whispered inside my head.

"Morning," Jackson said. My admiration couldn't be greater for the cool with which he uttered it. His is a manliness I aspire to, but know will always only be an aspiration.

I heard my brain stutter over whether to ask if she knew this was a men's locker room but by the time I realized she had to know it, Jackson was already conversing with her in a voice as slow and smooth as honey.

"Uh ... excuse me. Uh ... mind if I add some steam?" I asked eagerly, a little puppy just happy to be there even though I felt like a third-wheel. Jackson and the babe turned and looked at me as if my voice was the escape of an indiscrete noise.

"Uh ... okay then," I muttered and carefully stood up so as not to loosen my towel, pulled the hose as close to the thermostat as possible to avoid spraying cold water on either of them, then let it loose.

She sat on the ledge of the tile between us, much closer to Jackson than me, and turned just slightly toward him. Her exceptionally long, shapely leg crossed gracefully at the knee with a manicured foot a millimeter away from touching Jackson's bare shin.

I noticed for the first time she was wearing shiny red stiletto heels that matched the color of her polished toenails. The fog of steam allowed me to safely ogle from behind its veil and *elegant* was the word that came to mind. She had an elegant shape, an elegant and miniscule swimsuit, an elegant hairstyle and, my god, truly elegant legs. Her breasts peeked over the cups loosely holding them in, succulent and supple. I so much wanted to touch her flaxen hair, coiffed without looking dyed or stiff. In a word, she was stunning and though shocking to have any woman sitting there in the steam room, it was also this woman in particular that made it so bewildering. Yet Jackson chatted with her easily, and both of them giggled back and forth. In the halo of her beauty I succumbed happily to my role as Tonto, realizing my mouth was still hanging wide open at the supreme good fortune of the Lone Ranger.

"Excuse me, gentlemen," she said with a smile, and turned to nod at me for the first time, "but I much prefer the steam to kiss open my pores."

Then, her voice still singing in my morning brain and thoughts spinning from her intoxicating presence, she gracefully untied the top of her swimsuit and released her breasts into the freedom of the moist air. My stomach suddenly shot into my throat not to mention the movement that took place underneath my towel.

Jackson shook his head approvingly and let go a small understatement. "Nice."

Then, almost immediately, Jackson's eyes darted to track a motion outside the glass door. I saw it too. Suddenly the noise of the world outside the glass filled the steam room as the door opened. Laughter poured in as steam rushed out. For an instant I was frozen in confusion with no idea what was happening. I felt utterly naked under a spot light. Jackson laughed too and mixing with the guffaws from the other male voices the noise became thunderous.

Suddenly I remembered the bare breasts and tore my attention away from Jackson to the woman in red stilettos. She stood and laughed as well, even as she tied her top back on. It was clear everyone besides me knew what was going on.

Jackson seemed aware of my bewilderment and explained that the guys looking in were Detectives playing a practical joke on him for his birthday.

I laughed.

The feeling of being the butt of a joke evaporated immediately, but even so I held my towel tightly at the waist just in case.

Now I could see beyond the doorway and count a handful of cops and firefighters standing there in the area between the steam room and showers, all squeezed together to see inside the steam room. Someone shouted that she was a stripper they hired to lure him into thinking she was just another beautiful woman hitting on him. Jackson laughed so hard tears rolled down his cheeks. Wow, the dude was so much better of a sport than I would have been. If it had been me, I would have fallen hook, line and sinker, and they would have found me worshipping at her feet before the joke was sprung. But Jackson was suave and manly in the midst of the situation and my admiration for him almost reached the level of awe. Honestly, I envied him for it.

Man, I chuckled to myself, Wilson was going to shit his pants when I told him what he missed. I wished he had been there that morning. I missed him especially after all of it was over, when Jackson and his buds and the howls of laughter were suddenly gone and the quiet felt deadly.

I was left thinking about Jackson and his manliness. I thought about my sons who were approaching manhood. I wondered what I should tell them about being a man. Then again, for good or ill, I had already taught them everything I knew by example.

Still, what did I wish I had taught them? What was left to say? What should I tell them before it's too late?

Don't stop reading. That was the first thing I could think to tell them. It's tempting to quit reading when there is no teacher or professor requiring it but women don't seem to quit. At least not as many women as men quit reading.

Never stop remaking yourself. The world around them won't stop changing so if they stop changing it will turn them into brittle old men before their time.

Learn not to seek the love and approval of men or women. Instead, they need to seek the path and calling of their own life; and when they find it, authentic love and affirmation will be waiting there for them.

You are alone. I suddenly wanted to warn them that the gnawing suspicion deep inside is true, so they need to get good at enjoying their own company. If they can do that, then those fleeting moments of connection with others will be just so much gravy.

Say good-bye to your mother. It turns out that a deep and abiding sense of masculinity does depend upon a clean separation from mom, but healthy masculinity also depends upon being able to reconnect with her when the time is right.

Being wise is better than being smart. Creativity and the imagination are the single most important ingredients for the life of the mind, and the essential difference between smart and wise men.

Emotions are nutrients for the mind. Those strong emotions are intended for pleasure, growth and strength; so feel them, listen to them, experience them, and then digest and excrete them.

Sex is for bonding. I hope they will enjoy their body, enjoy their partner's body, and treat both with mutual kindness and respect.

You deserve to be treated well. They need to know that the body is not the temple of the soul; it is life itself – their very life, so treat it well and insist that others treat it well too.

Always stand up for those you love. For that matter, they need to stand up for themselves and what they believe also.

I repeated the list in my head and wondered if I could remember all of it when I left the chamber of deep thoughts? If I wrote it all down and gave it to my boys would they look at me like I'm nuts? Then it hit me that I had never talked to them about being men. I

111

The Steam Room Diaries

wondered if anyone had.

Chapter Thirteen

Gym Dates

There was a soft spot between Gina and Rebecca where I nestled every Monday morning. If I hadn't felt such affection for both of them, or worry about hurting their feelings by abandoning them, I would not have gone through the demanding exertion and painful entanglements required by our physical contortions together. Still, there is something about staying with the same partner for a long time that is especially pleasurable and compensates for all the obvious distress.

When I was running late on Monday mornings it was with the ease and comfort of knowing Gina and Rebecca would have saved me a place, tucked cozily between them.

Everyone but me in the class wore a skin tight top with a midriff gap of flesh that reached down to equally tight yoga pants. Whoever thought this was a good look should be punished by the fashion gods. The number of ordinary people who sport a stomach that should be viewed by the general public equals a spit in the ocean. Mine is well covered by a formerly white, now dingy t-shirt that proclaims "BALL STATE" in red letters above a smirking cardinal. My non-yoga motif matched a one-of-a-kind yoga mat I've had for a decade colored in the pattern of the green, black, and yellow Jamaican flag. Raggedy old sweatpants as baggy as I can find them, XXXLT, complete my early man-cave couture and accentuated the fact I was the only man in the Monday morning yoga class.

Every woman in the class, regardless of shape, size, or age, preferred one of the various styles of yoga pants without enough excess material to offer even a small wrinkle. I marveled at their lack of inhibition given the intolerable level of discomfort it causes me to have even an inch of fat or other imperfection exposed to the general public. None of those women had the kind of humongous bellies frequently seen shaking in the open air September through January at Buffalo Bills games, but some of them had a lot more than an inch to pinch.

Gina sported a mane of luxurious hair. It was not highly stylized in a slick coiffed look, but rather, cascaded with natural curls and waves of dark red. Her hair bounced and bobbed with each body motion yet somehow always landed in the same shape. The lavish tresses atop her head were in perfect proportion to the size of her face and body, and she was just lovely to look at. Her upper body was muscular while her lower body just fleshy enough to bounce a bit. This little give to an otherwise taut body was not surprising given she had her first of three children at age thirty-seven. Still, she was in great shape for a fifty year old with young children.

What I especially loved about Gina was her unvarnished authenticity. She would no more attempt to hide her little potbelly or droopy butt than she would rob a bank. Just the opposite, she reversed Bobby Knight's famous advice and practiced an exceptional offense as her best defense, often by pointing out to me the tidiest and roundest little bottoms in the class.

"Look at her ass," she'd whisper loudly from our perch in the back row. "I bet she hasn't had dessert since 9/11, and she probably works out three hours every day to have a curvaceous butt like that!"

Gina often made a big deal over Rebecca's firm, round derrière. In response Rebecca's face squirmed between a beaming smile and grimace, and sometimes both at once. Gina is loud, brassy and laughably neurotic. She was a nurse in her pre-mom life (or "BM Days" she called it, *before mom*), but Gina long since gave up any thoughts about the world beyond her three children, inattentive husband and massive, shedding Newfoundland puppy. Her world revolved around her children's needs: volunteering in their classrooms, making all the correct foods for the Jewish holidays, teaching her children Jewish customs for table worship, training the puppy, and scolding her husband.

Conversation with Gina was largely a non-stop commentary and litany of complaints about each one of her routine tasks. Just when the whining became intolerable, she said something hysterical and commanded uproarious laughter from everyone within earshot. Gina could describe in detail, with equal volume and verve, the number and degree of rippling abdominal sags she had left over from childbirth and how to make Loukoumades or Latkes.

All this contrasted vividly with Rebecca who was at least a decade younger than Gina, although she never told us her age. Rebecca had two small children too, a boy and a girl, who had already started school. She did not stay home with her children except for the employer-sanctioned period of maternity leave allowed for each. Rebecca had a career and worked as vigorously at succeeding in her profession as she did at maintaining her splendid butt.

I suspected she did everything with the same verve and ambition she threw into exercise: twenty minutes on the stair climber, followed immediately by twenty minutes on an elliptical machine, and finishing at the same high level of intensity with twenty minutes running on a treadmill at top speed with an onerous incline. After all of that she raced to the free-weights and pumped ten and twenty pound barbells to rhythms playing in her ear buds.

Rebecca was a driven woman.

She succeeded at everything she did, except relationships, which demanded far more attention and nuance than she had learned to offer or perceive. She had one of those faces that could appear soft and beautiful or sharp and disconcerting depending upon the light, angle, or whatever mysterious element renders such a contrast.

Gina and Rebecca were wonderful yoga and gym partners, each a kindred spirit in their own way and women with whom I would happily have shared the steam room if possible. It was even stranger then, that we nearly lost our friendship over their respective husbands.

As different as Gina and Rebecca were, both their husbands revealed they were having an affair with another women within thirty days of each other. The details in each case were sketchy, except for a strange coincidence: Rebecca's husband was having a tryst with a woman seven years older than him, while Gina's husband had chosen a woman younger by almost a decade.

The friendship between Gina and Rebecca was, as it turned out in the midst of their mutual ordeal, significantly mediated by my presence, even though it initially deepened as they shared the wounds of betrayal. After six years of exercising side by side, the dark tumult of philandering husbands provided us with our first occasion to meet outside of the gym.

During the trauma we met for coffee from time to time at a locally owned café. At these self-help sessions Gina and Rebecca unwrapped the unsavory details of disintegrating marriages to one another while I listened and commiserated. But over time a surprising turn of events took place. Gina, whom I would never have expected to strike out on her own, demanded a divorce. Rebecca, whom I worried might murder her husband in the dark of the night, went to couple's therapy and found a way to reconcile the relationship. The process of taking opposite directions began to pull them apart and I was left trying to navigate the middle.

It began slowly and tentatively, but little by little we stopped meeting for coffee and it wasn't long before each pulled me aside to say something about the other. Clearly something had to be done or these previously uncomplicated, comfortable as an old shoe relationships, would soon evaporate.

Dangerous and pernicious problems sometimes require extreme solutions, so I hatched a plot.

Gina had long been agitated by the inequity inherent in the men's locker room hosting a steam room while the women's locker room offered a perpetually broken sauna. I began by planting the seed of conspiracy in the fertile soil of Gina's resentment. I promised to sneak her into the men's locker room for a steam on a frigidly cold winter day, but only if Rebecca would come with us. Gina laughed about it at first, enjoying the simple fantasy as we imagined it out loud together. But Rebecca played the role of naysayer by asking practical questions about how in the world it could ever be done. Even telling her about the Stripper didn't mitigate her doubts.

Then one bitter day in January when Gina was nearing the end of her nasty, ugly divorce, I invited them both out for dinner. We went to Left Bank, a bohemian restaurant on the Westside of Buffalo where neither of them had ever been, and somewhere they were very unlikely to see any of their suburban neighbors. I ordered superb wine and they each drank enough to get silly, which is when I set the trap.

"It's supposed to be minus-seven tomorrow when we get up and windy as hell. A perfect morning for a steam!"

"You bettcha," Gina pounced.

"Oh, we're not on that old pipedream again, are we?" Rebecca answered dryly.

"Becca, I'll bet you fifty bucks Gina goes with me to the steam room tomorrow. How about it?"

"Are you serious," Rebecca hissed.

"Yeah, fifty bucks. I'll even go seventy-five."

"I'll throw in twenty-five," slurred Gina, "but until the divorce is final that's the best I can do."

"A hundred then," I declared triumphantly.

"Let me get this straight," Rebecca snorted incredulously. "You'll bet me one hundred dollars that Gina goes with you into the men's steam room tomorrow morning?"

"Yeah, one hundred bucks. But ... you have to go with us."

"You idiot," she retorted, "that's a stupid bet. You are saying that if she doesn't go into the men's steam room tomorrow then you two owe me a hundred bucks!"

"Yes, but you have to come with us to confirm it," I added with coyness dripping down my chin.

"Hmmm. Do I really think Gina will wake up tomorrow morning without blurry vision from all this wine and venture into the steam room?" Rebecca pondered.

As she thought about it Gina giggled into her wine glass.

"Okay, you're on. If you go in the steam room, Gina, and stay for at least five minutes, then I'll owe you one hundred dollars. If you don't go in, or if you just run in and run out, then you guys owe me one hundred dollars."

We all shook hands and laughed at one another's foolishness.

Yoga class came early with Rebecca and me sprawled on our mats on time, and Rebecca speculating that Gina's absence was her way of trying to void the bet. I stuck up for my partner in crime and eventually she arrived looking hung over and whispering loudly about how lousy she felt. The more we sweated the more we could smell alcohol on one another and the more it made us snigger in the back of the class. After class we rolled up our mats and excitedly reminded one another of the plan.

They were to go downstairs and put on a swimsuit, as I would also. After that they would enter the pool from the women's locker room and nonchalantly walk over to converse in front of the pool entrance to the men's locker room. With any luck, "Blondie" would be the lifeguard on duty that day because she was such an affable extravert who engages in loud conversations across the pool that she rarely pays attention to anything else. When the shower and steam room were clear, I would open the door that leads from the pool to the men's locker room. All Gina and Rebecca would have to do is casually back through the door without being noticed from the pool. Once inside, pool door to steam room was a very short ten-foot dash.

The plan worked perfectly, right down to Blondie wandering off in conversation with an old lady in a swim cap pulled down to her goggles. No one saw Gina and Rebecca disappear through the door. On my end the only person in the locker room was Dweedle who sat in his usual place reading the paper. Although Dweedle had a peripheral view of the steam room door from where he sat, his powers of observation were slim to none.

I cracked open the door and whispered their names. Immediately the door pushed in as the two women squeezed through, Gina giggled and Rebecca shushed her.

"Come on!" I whispered over my shoulder and felt Gina's hand squeeze the flesh of my collar as if I was the leader of a conga line.

We rushed in and immediately I grabbed the hose and pointed it at the thermostat, hoping a room full of steam would conceal our undercover operation. I can remember thinking, even as I sprayed the hose, that seeking safety in the steam was akin to hiding under a blanket for protection against something fierce.

Then, without warning, standing there like three teenagers in a small circle, the gurgling of the pipes promising steam, we looked at each other and broke out laughing. But seeing each other in swimsuits was also a little creepy, awkward in the same way as when we first saw each other in real clothes outside the gym. I tried to keep at bay the thought of getting kicked out of The COE for bringing two scantily clad women into the steam room. But nothing bad happened to Jackson and she was a stripper!

Still giggling nervously we sat down very close to one another at first, then thought better of it and spread out a bit. We felt the clock ticking. Gina gave the steam room a once over and pronounced it awfully small. Rebecca drolly critiqued it as not that clean. Then we settled back in our places talking and laughing and having a big old time, just as if we were next to one another upstairs on the elliptical machines. Suddenly the door opened and long tall Ted walked in wearing nothing but his birthday suit.

Rebecca screamed and covered her face.

"Oh my god, look how long that pecker is!" Gina exclaimed.

•　　•　　•

The friendship between Gina and Rebecca returned in earnest after the steam room escapade, and we used the hundred dollars to have a dinner together at Rue Franklin, the best French restaurant in Buffalo. The steam room caper became the talk of yoga class and the weight room. Maggie took a photograph of the three of us, fashioned it into a faux "Wanted" poster, and hung it near the front desk where it stayed for about eight months. Ted seemed unconcerned about his public showing and perhaps even a little proud of the notoriety.

My mother used to point out that if priests and ministers followed the constraints of their institutions, clergy would not be allowed to have true friendships. They would be completely dependent upon their families or the church for all their needs, my mother would caution, and she was right. The social isolation of clergy is all the more ironic when friendship is the balm that salves the wounds that otherwise destroy us.

When I am alone in the steam room and allow my mind to wander down the census of blessings in my life, friendship floats up near the top. Some people say that God is known in miracles but frankly, I have known God most intimately in friendships.

Chapter Fourteen

Frodo's Agony

It was 8:30 AM on a Tuesday and Frodo was still in the steam room? I must have lingered too long over coffee and newspaper at home, I thought to myself, and so will have to pay the price of Frodo's naked body parts making unpleasant noises and invading my peace of mind in that sanctuary.

Steam flowed in full force as I opened the door, which mitigated the full visual affront of Frodo's sit-ups and leg stretches. Still, steam can do nothing to mask the sound. Each time Frodo's lower back touched the ledge as he did sit ups, the moisture on the tile created suction and when his skin pulled away as he sat up, it broadcast something akin to the sound of a large fart. Upon my request, management had taped a sign to the outside of the glass door: Please, no shaving or exercising in the Steam Room. Asshole blurted into the silence of my thoughts before channeling my focus to assert mind over matter.

Suddenly Frodo sat up, pivoted on his butt to face in my direction, and dropped his legs so that his feet were planted squarely on the floor. I opened my eyes at the cessation of flatulence and the sound of motion.

"Do you have children," he asked with restrained urgency in his voice.

"Five, as a matter of fact," I said, a little unnerved to actually be in conversation with Frodo after all these years.

"Any girls?"

"Yeah, three."

"How old?"

I had to think for a minute, and felt under pressure, as if it was a test of my fatherhood.

"Fourteen ... uh, seventeen, and twenty-four."

"What's the twenty-four year old doing?"

I hesitated while deciding how much I wanted to censor or sculpt the truth. I like the word "sculpt" so much better than "spin" – one is artistic and the other mechanical. Somehow anything artistic promises more authenticity and integrity.

"Well, she graduated from the University of Chicago with a degree in physics, so of course she is now living a life of abject poverty in Guatemala doing something with water treatment."

"Yeah. Okay. So you know what it's like. Mine is in India following her Argentinean guru, only she still hasn't finished college."

"What's she into?"

"Man, you got me. I can't pronounce the names of the people or places, they're all in

Hindi or Spanish or – you know, I don't even know what language they are in. All I know is that when I ask her, she tells me this stuff that sounds like mush-mouthed mumbling, then smiles and shakes her head up and down in affirmation of all that she has just told me. I feel like I am supposed to wag my head up and down too but what I want to do is wag it left and right and say, 'No, no, no.'"

"You mean you don't know what her mentor teaches?"

"Yoga, I guess. But she goes from living in Argentina to India for months at a time, and moves from one ashram to the next. An ashram ..."

"Yeah, I know what an ashram is."

"So she goes from one to another and studies whatever the specialty of the ashram she's in. When I ask her what she wants to do for a living, you know, eventually, she just says she wants to learn as much as she can from her 'teacher.' 'Like what?' I ask her. She says she wants to learn about enlightenment and be a 'teacher' herself someday. Wow, like that is an option in life!"

"Yeah, that's a stretch."

I suddenly realized I was feeling years of aggravation and hidden hostility toward Frodo melt at the edges, the way ice cream oozes down the side of a waffle cone faster than you can lick it off.

"I figured you knew something about Eastern religion," Frodo confessed.

"Wow, how'd you figure that?" My surprise was genuine.

"I don't know, I watch and listen. You say things to people sometimes that make me think of Tuny – that's my daughter. We named her Tara but somewhere along the line her nickname became Tuny."

"Yeah, one of my daughters is Beetle, but that's a long story."

"Besides, you're always in here meditating or praying or something, rather than stretching or exercising like most of us. So I just figured maybe you knew something about Eastern religions."

"I just close my eyes, man. I'm not really meditating and praying. But I was a priest ..." It slipped out before I could take it back.

"I knew it!" Frodo had a look of victory on his face.

"We were talking about it last week, man, right there in the corner of the locker room. I said, 'I bet he's a priest or minister or something!'"

"*Was,*" I said, trying to sound matter-of-fact when an enema of panic rose up from the tile beneath my ass. "I *was* a priest, now I am nothing. I don't mean nothing, I mean, now I'm like everyone else. Actually, that's not what I meant to say either, because priests are just like everyone else too. But anyway, I was a priest and now I'm not."

"Was it sex, man?"

"No, at least not exactly. It wasn't child

sexual abuse or anything. It wasn't even an affair. I did fall in love with a woman but we never had sex before I left the priesthood. So it wasn't exactly sex the way most people would think about it. It was love ... then it was sex."

"It's always the sex, man. It's crazy the Church thinks guys can live without it and not get weird. I feel your pain."

No he doesn't. He didn't hear a thing, I said to myself.

"No, really, it wasn't sex. And some people can do celibacy, but honestly, not that many can do it well. Anyway, I became a Protestant minister after I left the Roman Catholic Church, and we got married, which is when I came to fully appreciate sex."

"That's a rip, man. Most guys forget what sex is like when they get married." This brought a torrent of loud, staccato laughter shooting out of Frodo's mouth. Then he asked me, "So, like, can you tell me what my daughter is into with this Eastern religion stuff?"

"Well ... um, not really, not without talking to her or knowing anything specific," I said. "I can describe a basic difference between Eastern and Western religion, if that would help?"

Frodo eagerly nodded so I continued.

"In much of Eastern religion it is believed that the spiritual wisdom people seek can be taught and practiced, so if you engage in it long enough and with enough patience and discipline, you will be transformed in some way. In the West, religion is based upon 'revelation.' That means spiritual wisdom can only come from God. In other words, no matter how much we practice there is nothing we can do to 'get' a revelation if God isn't offering it. Western religions believe that the *revelation* is what transforms and it is not accessible by any individual, only received as a gift. That's a big difference. Your daughter is looking for knowledge and wisdom she believes is accessible with practice."

"Yeah, huh? I never heard that before." Frodo gets quiet. "So ... Tuny is trying to be transformed into something or someone else?"

"Like I said, I don't know what religion your daughter is practicing but I suspect learning to detach from false attachments such as wealth, beauty, and status is probably part of her practice. Speaking of which, how does she get money to travel?"

"She comes home and works for a few months. She's incredible, really. She can get a waitressing or bartending job at almost any of the really good restaurants in town because they love her. She'll make a couple thousand bucks and go back. She says she can live really well on seventy dollars a week in India. I worry about what kind of squalor she is living in and if she's safe."

"Maybe you ought to go visit her over there and that way you can see for yourself, then you might not be so worried. I've been to India and believe me she can live in a very nice place for that kind of money, and eat well too. Or at least she could before the recent boom they've been having. She's not living in the comfort of what you and I are used to but if she is ashraming, she's used to a very different standard."

Frodo's face wrinkled in a way I had never seen before. In fact, it dawns on me now that I never actually looked deeply into his face before. In the blink of an eye I could see the haggard look of a worried father where before I attributed to Frodo only the plasticized quest for youthfulness, a narcissistic staring into the mirror to make sure the muscles were cut just right.

Looking at him then, I recognized I had been projecting. For years he had been nothing but a living movie screen for the projection of my own assumptions, fears and prejudices.

"She would like that," Frodo snapped with an exclamation. "Why didn't I think of that before? Of course I could visit her in India. It may not be my first choice for a vacation, but what the hell?"

"You'll never be the same."

"Ha! I bet that's right!" he laughed with a new lightness.

"Do you have a wife or partner?" I asked, feeling ashamed that I had always told myself he was gay for reasons that suddenly seemed deeply bigoted.

"Yes, I'm married, why?" he asked flatly.

"Because you should go alone," I cautioned.

He looked at me quizzically, so I add quickly, "If you go alone, you and your daughter will deepen your relationship like never before. She will delight in showing you her life, and she will feel wowed and special because you came all that way by yourself, just to see her, and discover her world."

Then, thinking about what I just said, I blurted out, "But there would be nothing wrong if you went with your wife, either. That'd be cool too. It's just, well, I have found that when I have discovery trips one-on-one with my kids, it can be magical the way it enriches the relationship. But either way, you're in for a treat. Just do it, man."

"By God, I will!" Frodo jumped to his feet as if ready for action. He shook my hand and disappeared through the door which had barely shut before Frodo re-entered.

"Name's Pete, what's yours?"

I nodded. "Craig, but everyone calls me Spin."

Just then the fire alarm went off and we both jumped higher than is good for two middle-aged men to do.

"Oh shit!" I yelled, trying to remember if I had any clothing I could put on quickly. Since 9/11 everyone around The COE took those drills seriously. The "Lackawanna Six"[1] made people in the area a bit jumpy and the center staff required members to play through the drills with a deadly serious face.

By the time I got my sweats, socks and shoes haphazardly pulled on my wet body, the only one left in the locker room was Dweedle who was still putting on shoes and looking a little rattled. I ran around the corner and yelled back over my shoulder for Dweedle to hurry up. Halfway down the hall I stopped. *What if this really was a fire and I left an 80-something year old man in the locker room by himself?*

I went back and waited for Dweedle, and together we walked up the stairs. As we finally reached the top step, just in front of the desk where Maggie sits, everyone was already coming back into the building.

"We're toast!" I said to Dweedle. "If that had been a real fire or bomb we'd be under it!" I half laughed.

Dweedle took my arm, squeezed it and said, "Thanks for walking with an old man."

---

[1] The first post 9/11 prosecutions of US nationals for Al Qaeda-related crimes were in the metropolitan area of Buffalo.

Chapter Fifteen

Welcome Socrates

The ancient Greek philosopher, Socrates, believed that everything there is to know could be known or discerned by an inquisitive mind standing within the confines of one's own city. In other words, you do not have to travel the world or go very far in order to know what is worth knowing.

Socrates didn't leave Athens and I read somewhere that Jesus never traveled more than eighty miles from where he was born. In fact, none of the sages of antiquity were world travelers or sophisticated in the ways we might require of them today.

I thought about Socrates as I pulled into myself surrounded by noise and banter in the steam room.

In principle, I should have been able to retreat to the small moist place and travel no farther in order to plumb the depths of human wisdom. But I am not Socrates.

The closest we have to a *Steam Room Socrates* sat at the other end of the bench from me, surrounded by his former henchmen. Stevenson was the sage of the men's locker room and whenever he was present the steam room would be transformed into his Salon. The steam room was never more crowded than when Stevenson held forth and thus the reason for my need to back inside myself as far as possible. The latest political scandal or election-cycle scenario, or even just plain local gossip, swirled in the air around Stevenson.

He was as skinny as a pinstripe, still sleek and mostly taut in his eighties, and he sported a year-round tan with an accent of silver puff pastry hair. He pastured in Phoenix during the winter with his handsome middle-aged wife who refused to leave the sunshine for Western New York. Returning by himself to live in his South Buffalo haunt for the duration of the city's idyllic Camelot summers and now retired from public life, Stevenson was both famous and infamous in the region.

His extended family ruled the political roost for thirty years, holding the reins of patronage and ward politics, and doled out Block Grants and HUD money like candy to loyal minions and pay-to-play entrepreneurs alike. "The Clan," as it was known in the old days, survived one federal and state investigation after another only to emerge unscathed even as numbers of its cronies went to jail.

Stevenson's brother was an eight-term mayor and two of his uncles were judges. Even today the police and fire departments are rife with vestiges of The Clan, although they are vanishing with each succeeding class of retirees. The "Southies" as the denizens of South Buffalo are called, were defeated by a disciplined African-American organization that sprang up in the late twentieth century. The new regime is called "The Root" and has controlled the city and purse strings of power ever since. Toward the very end of their reign, a few peripheral members of The Clan went to jail as a pretense of reform. Unwittingly, by accident even, Stevenson was one of them.

Even though Stevenson was already living in Phoenix at the time, he remained on the city payroll using an abandoned cottage in the Fredrick Law Olmstead designed Central Park as his local mailing address. His fraud might have gone unnoticed if he hadn't gotten crossways with The Root organization, but that was inevitable since Stevenson was renowned for racist rhetoric and vindictiveness.

A patron of The Root was placed in management over a section of the Parks Department that formerly reported to Stevenson. The move was forced by a growing majority of Root members elected to the City Council, and against the wishes of Stevenson's brother, Mr. Mayor. Stevenson was not shy about broadcasting his resentment or his prognostications that the African American then in charge of park maintenance was not up to the job.

Stevenson, it is popularly believed, had

Clan employees poison every one of the eighteen greens in the Central Park Golf Course. Not only did the greens turn black but after a torrential rain, the runoff into the manicured lake in the middle of the park caused a massive fish kill. An investigation turned up evidence that Stevenson was behind the event, and that led to the fact that his actual domicile was in Phoenix, which in turn unraveled a whole series of other illegal shenanigans. Stevenson was the only member of the mayor's family to actually do time.

Looking at Stephenson holding court with guys who used to work for him, I fell back into the memory of my first ever visit to the steam room. It was during my first week in Buffalo, and there was Stevenson. I was by myself in the steam room wondering how to make the steam turn on when Stevenson entered.

"How 'bout steam?" He reached for the hose and demonstrated the unique method for turning up the heat.

"Basketball?" was all he asked, as if that said it all.

"Yeah, long time ago," I answered.

"Post?"

"What else?"

"Well they make guards your size these days," he answered.

"Yeah, well, they did back then too, which is why I didn't get very far."

"I've seen you play upstairs. You move

pretty well for an old guy. You must have had good feet."

"Yeah, I exceeded expectations. Opponents always underestimated me, which worked to my advantage. You play?"

"Coached. 'Course I played too, when it was still a white man's game."

"Where'd you coach?" I asked.

"Semi-pro. We won three national championships when I was there."

"Wow." I acted impressed. Who knew semi-pro played national championships?

"Where'd you play?" he asked.

"High school ball, in Indiana."

"Indiana!" Now it was his turn to be impressed. "Outside of New York City, that part of the country is basketball Mecca. Bob Knight, Larry Bird, Gene Keady, Hoosiers, those guys understood the game and they handled their players the way they should be handled."

So the conversation went.

I saw Stevenson almost every day that summer without knowing a thing about him. He never talked about his public life or much of anything other than basketball, a subject neither one of us could ever exhaust. Then, when I didn't see him for several weeks I asked around about him in the locker room and that is when I found out he lived in Phoenix from October to May. It was then I began to hear the infamous stories and witticisms carried by the wings of oral tradition.

Poof! The noise of laughter and old Buffalo brogue extinguished my soft envelope of memory. I was coerced back into the moment by the volume of the voices.

Stevenson and his cohort that day consisted of two other old guys I didn't know and Ted. Ted is friends with Stevenson's granddaughter – "the wild one" Stevenson calls her.

"She'll take every bit of what you got down there, Ted." Stevenson pointed to Ted's crouch. "And then ask for more," he said with a straight face as his buddies snorted. Ted blushed.

"How's Bunny?" one of the old guys inquired.

"Bitch. She up and left me for some rich bastard who's got a bigger house and a bigger boat. At least the divorce was in Arizona instead of New York."

"Fuckin' A!" one of the other old guys shouted. "New fuckin' York'll freaking rape a man and give a bitch anything she asks for."

"You didn't just let her go, did you Stevie?" the guy asked incredulously.

"Yeah, no revenge," Stevenson said without a care in the world.

"What happened to you, Stevie? In the old days you'd a had someone cut her face or something," the bigger of the two sidekicks grimaced.

I shuddered trying to put the Stevenson I

knew from one-on-one basketball talk with this guy's Stevenson.

"That was then, Sparks." He grinned. "Got religion."

Both old guys laughed as if this was a joke and Ted gurgled a forced chuckle so as to fit in. But Stevenson looked back at the old guys with shark eyes.

"I got religion," he said again. "If you got religion, you don't go after folks, you forgives 'em. The bitch's got my forgiveness. That's all."

The old guys didn't know what to say. They looked at one another and back at Stevenson, whose gaze was toward the floor. No one said anything. Finally Ted tiptoed up to the subject.

"You mean you go to Church and have a priest down there," Ted whispered.

"No, I told you, I got *religion*. Forget Catholics, bunch of child molesters and embezzlers. I go to a real church, a Bible Church. The preacher talks sense and the music is good and they don't do all that ritualistic folderol. It's just the Bible, and Jesus as he really is. You guys outta try it."

Again silence fell like a thud around us. I liked it. The old guys looked down at the filthy wet floor and Stevenson glanced around trying to catch someone's gaze, to look them straight in the eyes employing offense as the best defense. Mine were the only eyes

Stephenson's met.

"He knows what I'm talking about," Stevenson said motioning to me. Now they all looked at me and Stevenson told them I was from Indiana and played basketball, and speculated if anywhere had the real old time religion, it was Indiana.

"Am I right?" he goaded me.

"Well ... there is certainly a lot of that kind of religion back there, but they got ordinary Catholics and Protestants too." Then, as a second thought I asked, "You speak in tongues at this church you go to?"

"Hell no. Just good old fashioned Bible preaching."

"How do you get forgiveness in a Church like that if you don't have priests and sacraments?" Ted seemed to be wondering out loud.

"You don't need no goddamn priest to get saved!" Stevenson snarled with a bitterness that seemed grounded in something personal.

"You ask for it directly when you take Jesus as your personal Lord and Savior. You don't need anyone standing between you and the Almighty, except Jesus. Catholics – Shit," he barked.

"You're whole family's Catholic, Stevie," one of the old guys whined like a kicked dog.

"Yeah, well they're superstitious too. You think when I was in jail I got one visit from a Catholic chaplain? You think when I got out of prison, Fr. Hennessy was there to greet me and welcome me back into the parish? You think Bishop Hammer, who was happy to give me whatever I wanted when I could do him favors, ever called to see how I was doing? Once I could no longer take Catholic Charities over the top at the end of their campaign, I was nothing to them. My preacher down in Phoenix never once asked me for money, the Church up here never once asked for anything that wasn't connected to money."

"Your mom is turning over in her grave," one of the old guys stammered as he looked nervously at Stevenson and then to the ground.

"I figure my mom's got it all figured out by now, and she can see that what I'm doing is right. I'm right with Jesus and I'm right with God. That's all I know."

"Hey, Indiana," he blurted out, grabbing my attention and pulling me out of my shell. "Tell them! Tell 'em all you need is Jesus and the Bible, right?"

The old guys and Ted stared at me, waiting for an answer. I sat for a moment thinking about Socrates.

Socrates, rather than deny the truth as he understood it, accepted the form of capital punishment for what those in power considered sedition. He drank the prescribed poison in a third century BCE version of intravenous execution. Socrates was accused of debunking the gods of his day, or more specifically, corrupting the youth by subverting their faith in the official religion of Athens. What would Socrates, I wondered, make of Stevenson's abandonment of his ethnically rooted family religion in favor of the pop-culture religion of his current social milieu?

"Well ... I need a lot more than Jesus and the Bible, myself. A good woman, some good friends, and rare prime rib now and again," I quipped.

They all laughed, even Stevenson.

"I think, maybe, God is bigger than the boxes we put God in," I continued on the soapbox, the one Stevenson had handed me. "The Catholic box, the Bible box, the Buddha box – they are all several sizes too small for God. That doesn't mean they aren't any good, just that none of them has it all. That's what it seems like to me, anyway."

"Well I'll be goddamned, Indiana, if you don't sound like some kind of a steam room Buddha." Stevenson laughed. The old guys joined in with Ted bringing up the rear just to make sure he stayed plugged in.

•　　•　　•

The next day when I got to the steam room, the first news was from Dweedle. Stevenson had died the night before crossing the street in front of his house. They said it was a hit and run, but speculation ran deep that it was an old grudge.

They laid him out at Amigone Funeral Home and then held a Mass for the Repose of the Soul at Fourteen Holy Helpers Church. It had all the Catholic trimmings Stevenson had come to hate, and everyone talked in muted tones about all the good he did for the City of Buffalo.

Afterward, at the wake, there was lots of drinking and laughing and stories old and new about the Stevenson everyone knew. I don't do funerals much anymore but I went to Stevenson's, just out of respect for the community of the steam room.

My feelings about Stevenson are complicated. There was so much about him I could not respect and didn't like. But there was an additional part of him, the little slice of his life that was a summer of days in the steam room, during which he was kind and pleasant.

Socrates comes back to mind: "Bad men live that they may eat and drink, whereas good men eat and drink that they may live."[2]

Somewhere along the way, Stevenson may have gone from one to the other. I shouldn't admit it, but remembering that Stevenson called me the steam room Buddha still makes me grin inside. Remembering the sound of Stevenson's laugh makes me grin too.

---

[2] Plutarch's Morals--How a Young Man Ought to Hear Poems

144

Chapter Sixteen

Dirty Children

A short night and a short workout but I am alone in the steam room.

My middle daughter came home hours past her curfew last night and I waited anxiously and angrily until she arrived at four in the morning. *I am too old for this*, I heard myself grimace as I finished spraying the sensor and leaned against the wall with legs stretched out on the ledge. I had to guard against falling asleep because staying in there too long would do bad things to my heart. Estefan opened the door and I relaxed a bit knowing his annoying presence would keep me awake.

Estefan bowed his head in a small, silent gesture of recognition. I bent mine right back at him, also without sound. At opposite ends we sat in silence with the steam enveloping us.

While it was blessedly silent I caught myself studying Estefan.

Everything about him squeaks of compulsive order and neatness with one exception. His lavish head of hair was perfectly groomed, as well as his flagrant matching white mustache. He owned a tidy, trim torso with very little body hair and no distinguishing marks. Any time I had seen him dressed, it was without a wrinkle or unbuttoned flap. The lone rebellion from this otherwise orderly aura was wrapped around his left wrist.

There, in no apparent order and frayed to varying degrees, were four or five small, colorful and clearly hand-woven bracelets. It was this chaotic dissonance of threads upon which my stare lodged. Suddenly I snapped back from my thickheaded stupor unsure of how long I had been staring or if Estefan had caught me.

Still the colorful phalanx of bracelets attracted my attention. One was cobalt blue and canary yellow in an intricately twisted weave; another purple and orange, still another black and yellow. Each one appeared to been woven in a different pattern and with different colors, although one was all black with what looked like a few small wooden beads woven into it. None of them looked spanky clean and new. They were unraveling unevenly but all in decline. One of them was so scraggly it looked like a baby goat umbilical waiting to fall off.

"You like them?" he asked, wriggling his wrist just a little.

"Oh," I said, startled and embarrassed. "Yeah, uh, nice. I was just wondering where you got all those," I lied. I was actually just spacing out in my sleep-deprived stupor and if anything, wondering about the dissonance of the raggedy bracelets with the squeaky Estefan.

"Where did you get them?" I asked as I cleared my throat.

"Well, let me tell you the story," he said with disconcerting eagerness.

"Last summer I was in Antigua, Guatemala with a friend. Maybe you know him because he is at the college too. Dr. Zachary Waddles?"

"Hmmm," I searched the vagary of my thickening thoughts and found a face to go with the name. "Yes, I know him." I smiled as if winning at cards.

"Yes, right. Well, one day we were sitting in our favorite late afternoon watering hole having a beer, smoking cigars, and talking about religion. Zachary teaches religion, you know, and so we often ended up talking about Church."

I shook my head in acknowledgement and hung on listening as best I could with sleep-deprived brain.

"There was another Gringo in the bar smoking a cigarette and drinking a beer, and suddenly he was surrounded by a passel of dirty children. They were selling stuff – bracelets like these," he said, holding up his wrist again and rolling it one way and another. "They were made out of wood, cloth and who-knows-what-else."

"How much?" I asked just to show I was still awake.

"They wanted 20 Quetzals for a bracelet, or about $2.75 US, but the cost is beside the point. Zachary and I were engrossed in our conversation about something or other and completely absorbed in the moment. Suddenly the three children swiftly surrounded us."

"'?Quieres compras un la pulsera?' or something like that," Estefan added sheepishly, "because I don't think my conjugation is right. 'Did we want to buy a bracelet,' they asked with big eyes."

"Gracias, no gracias," I said with considered politeness. Literally, without skipping a beat, the three boys hustled away to find another customer as Zachary and I went on with our conversation.

Estefan got up with slow deliberation as was his manner, never interrupting his story and walking over to where I sat. He turned on the spigot and with his ass nearly in my face, trained the spray of water on the thermostat.

"Three or four minutes passed," he reported while dropping the hose, "when the other Gringo ambled over our way and said, 'I heard you talking about Church.'"

Estefan walked back to his seat and said, "Zachary and I looked up at the gentleman and smiled. I pulled a chair out, making a motion as if for him to have a seat. Instead, all of a sudden he scowled and barked: 'You think Jesus would have said, Gracias, no gracias to those boys?'"

"And then," Estefan said before he paused a bit too long for my comfort, "he turned a funky little pirouette, and was gone before either Zachary or I could pick up our jaws."

"How rude," I commiserated.

"It wasn't just *what* he said," Estefan snapped and we both looked toward the gurgling pipes as steam shot up from the slated wood. "It was the *way* he said it; the tonal quality of his voice that was at one and the same time ghostly familiar and agitating. It was the tone of a *Church-hater*. You know the type." He looked at me and seemed to be taking a lot for granted. "Someone who has honed his resentments toward organized religion into a finely sharpened blade."

"It was, I suspected," Estefan reasoned, "from his point of view, the perfect opportunity to shed light on the hypocrisy of those of us who claim to follow Jesus. There we were, two Churchgoers full of ourselves talking about religion and Christianity, and we couldn't even recognize Jesus when he stood there selling bracelets to us. If those little boys weren't *Jesus*, the inference went, then they were at least some of those little *lambs* Jesus told us to take care of."

Unbeknownst to Estefan, I did know that sensation. It is being caught in a sting when you're not really one of the bad guys but happen to be in the wrong place at the wrong time, looking guilty, and knowing it. Squeezed in the small space between an emotional double exposure, anger and guilt are superimposed on one another even though you've done nothing wrong.

"So Zachary and I sat there and debriefed the experience, sorting out the complexity of it the way scholarly people do; we unpacked the stinging smear of the anti-church guy from what we knew about the world and Jesus."

I was suddenly aware of an odd sensation, and I had to figure out if that was actually affection or something else I was feeling for Estefan in spite of all his aggravating little behaviors? Was it the fog of steam melting all the years of consternation and disgust?

"Here is how we figured it," he said in an academic high tone.

"Both of us were seasoned travelers in Central America. We knew that often children who sell things on the street are actually victims themselves of some dark exploitive godfather who forces them to go out and sell, and then extracts from them everything they make – *keeping them* as a pimp uses violence to keep his prostitutes. It is not beneficial to anyone but the godfather to support that kind of a shadowy economy."

He looked over to make eye contact, wondering perhaps if I understood what he was talking about, which, being familiar with street scenes in the developing world, I was.

"We also understood that sometimes the kids who sell things are wonderfully expert pick-pockets," he went on. "But most importantly, even if buying from the children was the right thing to do in every respect, we were in Guatemala for three weeks and couldn't afford to support every vendor or beggar we encountered – there were thousands.

"Finally, we reflected on the passive-aggressive behavior of the guy who dumped on us and left. We reckoned the *real* Jesus would have pulled up a chair, engaged us in conversation, and deepened our understanding. The man in *our* story seemed more interested in vomiting resentments than encouraging our transformation."

I shook my head in complete sympathy.

"Thus" Estefan concluded a bit triumphantly, "we dissected the disturbing event, cleaned ourselves off, so to speak, and moved on. But ..." he added with too much drama, "I did change my behavior."

"How so?"

"Well, not really changed it, so much as became more intentional. You see, prior to that encounter I gave change to beggars and bought little things from kids here and there, but it was haphazard. The truth is, in that kind of economy, and a tourist, we avoided coins. The exchange rate was eight Quetzals to one dollar, so pockets soon burgeoned into saddlebags with coinage. What I did was buy a change purse and instead of avoiding change I stockpiled it; even going out of my way to get change. Then I made it my goal to never say 'Gracias, no gracias' and to always have at least one coin to give away."

Just then Hamm opened the door, saw that the two of us had the primo places, calibrated whether or not there was room for him to sprawl on the ledge in the middle, thought better of it, and closed the door without a word.

"Now if you have ever been in a developing country," Estefan continued his lecture, "especially in an urban area away from resorts and tourists, then you know how lofty a goal it was to always have a coin to give. We walked everywhere in Guatemala, and every street and alley has someone on it that asks for money. 'Si,' instead of 'Gracias, no gracias,' is ambitious to say the least."

I nodded in full agreement and realized I was cruising on a second wind, my thick-headedness thinning.

"But," he paused and it hit me for the first time that Estefan inserted those dramatic breaks frequently and was as much a drama queen as he was compulsively tidy.

"But lo and behold, from that day on, maybe eighty percent of the time, I said 'Si' and gave away something instead of 'Gracious, no gracious.'"

"Wow," I said with automatic expression.

"Oh, but here is the best part." Then he paused again. "On my last day in Guatemala, I had an hour to kill before getting picked up for the airport so I walked half a mile to La Merced, a 17th century monastery that makes even the largest church in Buffalo look like a little country chapel. There were baptisms going on up front so I sat in the rear pews. It felt like I was two miles from the altar shrouded in a massive pillared sanctuary."

As Estefan described the architecture I closed my eyes to envision it, drawing upon a slew of memories of churches and cathedrals I had visited in Central America.

Frodo opened the door and looked in. The steam was beginning to evaporate and drip heavily off the walls and ceiling. Frodo stepped toward the faucet, looked at us both and asked, "Mind if I make some steam?"

We both nodded our assent without words and Frodo gave it a little spray before sitting cross-legged on the ledge between Estefan and me. It struck me how he really did evoke the image of a Hobbit.

"Anyway, I just sat there for a while," Estefan continued without backing up the story for Frodo. "I was hovering in a state somewhere between thought and prayer, and drifting in and out of reflection on my time in Guatemala, and maybe even praying for those who had showed me hospitality. Then I stood and turned to leave.

"Immediately I saw a dark figure on the

floor huddled in the shadows just inside of the massive front doors. Really, it could have been a heap of rags for all I knew but I suspected there was a human in there somewhere. I felt around in my pocket for change and there it was, quite a lot of it."

The way we were positioned along the benches of the steam room I found myself having to look around Frodo to see Estefan so I kept my eyes closed and visualized the story in great detail, with colors and textures and even the scent of dust and mold of old churches.

"I took out two coins, one to bring home for each of my kids, and the rest I held in my hand for whoever was there under those rags in the shadow. Approaching the open church doors, light revealed the contour of a body. Soon I could see a man in his twenties or thirties who was missing both legs. As it turned out he was not huddled either. His posture and demeanor seemed almost relaxed, more composed than despairing."

I opened my eyes to see Frodo listening too, and then descended back into my own inner vision.

"As I got up close to him I could see his face. It was remarkably clear and clean," Estefan said in a newly hushed voice. "It almost shined," he whispered.

The steam room was closeted in stillness as the word "shined" evaporated into the vapor fogging the air between us, no sound emanated from outside the sweating glass door.

"The hair on his head and his beard were handsomely dark. His eyes, which were far more noticeable than the absence of his legs, were brilliant. I placed the coins into his bowl, or maybe it was his hand, I don't remember; but his eyes were locked onto mine when he said: 'Que Dios te bendiga.' I think that's what it was, but I *swear*, his Spanish pressed itself into my English and somehow I knew it meant, 'May God bless you.'"

Estefan was suddenly a pinch more animated, just a little more jumpy. It was not enough to jolt me out of my own imagination of events but it hurried me enough that I didn't linger with the visions inside my head.

"I tell you, in that man's eyes was the brilliance of *a god,* the spiritual strength of a Jesus or Mohammed. Perhaps I only saw what I wanted to see, or maybe I was just projecting my own stuff onto him and the situation, but I don't think so. Even now, even with distance, I don't think so."

For the first time in what seemed like several minutes I opened my eyes and returned to the steam room. Frodo's head was tilted down and he stared at the floor while Estefan shifted to sit more erect. He was talking with his hands and with an intensity I had suspected from Estefan all along but never witnessed before.

"I don't know if giving money to beggars

and panhandlers is the right or wrong thing to do, everyone has a different piece of that argument. But here is what I know now that I didn't feel before I met that legless man at the door: practice abundance when surrounded by scarcity. Everyone seems so worried about not having enough but how much is enough? You know what I mean?"

And then after another small pause he concluded. "So these bracelets, I bought them from one of those same boys in the bar, only it was a few days later on the street. They remind me to practice abundance."

"Now there's an idea you don't hear espoused every day!" I exclaimed.

Estefan smiled, got up, opened the door with one hand and saluted us with the other. "Que Dios te bendiga," he said as the door closed behind him.

"You want some more steam?" I asked Frodo.

"Sure, that would be great," Frodo answered as he stretched out to begin naked exercises.

I sprayed the pipes, turned off the water, dropped the hose and bid Frodo adieu, "Que Dios te bendiga."

Chapter Seventeen

Don't Steal No Cheeseburger!

Wilson once spent three months in the Erie County Jail for stealing a McDonald's cheeseburger and a medium coke.

He was nineteen and high and casually swiped some guy's meal on the way out of the fast food joint as a macho lark. His real mistake was having a lark in the suburb of Amherst where they don't like people from the city, especially African American males, coming out to their pristine community and adding crime statistics to their precious "Safest Town in America" profile.

"They do shit in there tha'd curl your hair, Big Man, if'n you had any. If'n you had any."

Wilson occasionally repeats his last phrase, what seems like a thought-stutter. There is no pattern to it; instead the repetition just jumps in at the last moment and plops down at the end of a sentence.

"Like what kind of shit?" I wanted to know, a voyeur from privilege, curious to hear how the other eighty-nine percent lives.

"You give 'em lip and they take you down to the service elevator in the back of the building, 'cause they got no security cameras in the elevator. It's not that big in there either, and you handcuffed, and you ankles is chained, and you get three or four fat mutha fuckar sheriffs squeezed in around you, and they slam you and stun you and use the rubber hose on you. And they're laughing the whole time. You try to keep from screaming or crying, and all the time they just laugh'n it up big. They just laugh'n it up big.

Wilson wasn't smiling.

Though he almost always smiled, he was not smiling as he remembered the experience.

He sat there with his cement block legs and shoebox feet planted flat on the floor, wagging his head back and forth, and making a sound a grandmother might if she wanted you to feel bad for what you just did: "Mmm, mmm, mmm."

I wasn't used to Wilson without a smile. It was the first time he told me anything about himself and I felt awkward with the gift, holding it but not knowing what to say.

"My cousin Mini was in overnight onest. She was seven months pregnant and one of the guards knocked her down. Knocked her down right to the floor. You believe that?"

"Nothing surprises me anymore," I said scowling with authority as if I had seen the suffering of the world and lived to tell about it. I didn't want Wilson to know the only jail cell I ever saw was on tour.

"My very first day in Buffalo," I sniffed,

maybe puffing up a little too much, "I went to work early and there were two of Buffalo's Finest beating up a drunk outside the door of my office. Right there on Main Street! The entire world could see and they didn't care. I stood there staring at them, figuring they would have to stop with a citizen watching but they just kept hitting the guy with clubs, and kicking him. Now and again one of them would look up at me as if to say, 'What you gonna a do about it?' The drunk was on the ground moaning and pleading for them to stop, and one of the cops kicked him and snarled, 'Shut up.'

"You take that inside, man, in Lock-up, behind closed doors, and in dere you at their mercy. It's no wonder people be hanging dem selves in there." Wilson said it shuddering, the memory of it shivering down his body until he caught himself then snapped back to a street demeanor of indifference to abuse.

Wilson was in his mid-thirties and lived in one of the Art Lofts that Hilary Clinton procured congressional funding for during her brief tenure as a Senator. He wrote rap lyrics and was a studio musician for recording artists, people with monikers I'm supposed to recognize. I acted impressed to hide my cultural ignorance.

He had a wife and kids; the oldest he took to a football program all the way out in Orchard Park, the suburban home to the Buffalo Bills. He said it's the best "fundamentals" program in the area and denigrated the city leagues because they didn't teach fundamentals. Stevenson would have liked Wilson if he were white.

It was rare for a Western New Yorker to be recruited for a Division I athletic program but Wilson had been one of the few. Recruited by Ohio State, Nebraska and Syracuse, he accepted a full ride to OSU. Then, as I said before, he blew out his knee the summer after his senior year.

Wilson never found another opportunity to go to college but he didn't look back longingly or with the slightest hint of regret. He cops that muscular male attitude that it's just the way it is, and so you move on. All the more striking that he broke his cool about the Erie County Jail. Talking about that experience cut furrows in his forehead that wrinkled deeply.

"Why they gotta be like that, Big Man?"

He looked at me straight in the eyes as if I could give him the answer. It created chaos in my thoughts as they raced through my brain.

God, does he think I know? Do I know? Am I supposed to know because I am one of them, or related to one of them? Is he looking into my eyes because he thinks I have some secret knowledge that will never be his? I probably do know the answer but take so much for granted that I can't see it. I don't even know that I know!

The silence between us seemed forever. The ground around us was littered with life below the surface and an invisible gulf opened between Wilson and me.

Buffalo is divided at Main Street, or should I say, the white and black neighborhoods of Buffalo are divided at Main Street. One side is bustling while the other side looks like Detroit. On one side graceful neighborhoods are tucked into the folds of a park system designed by Frederick Law Olmstead while on the other side, block after block a scarred prairie rolls out a landscape of abandoned warehouses and failed commercial strips. They clear the streets to the pavement in winter on one side of Main Street while the other side has potholes that get bigger and bigger from one winter to the next. One side has car jackings and drive-by shootings while the other side has sidewalk cafés and nightlife. Suddenly I felt as if I was on one side of Main Street looking over at Wilson who was standing on the other side.

I looked back at Wilson who stared at me as if we were lined up at opposite sides of a yard marker on the football field. He never blinked. My throat suddenly felt dry as a pot shard.

"I don't know, Wilson. My mom used to say that bullies are desperately trying to fill up a void inside by diminishing other people, which is ironic since she was a bully herself. Maybe people like that are shoveling shit into their own bottomless pit thinking that someone else's humiliation is going to make them feel better about it."

"What," he jerked with a loud voice as if I just slapped him. "Why you talking about bullies and shit?"

Back inside my head I began to panic. *Oh my god, our conversation must have moved on but the one in my head hasn't.*

Bewilderment was screwed on Wilson's face, his mouth twisted and half open, his eyes squinting into slits.

Okay, what was he saying before I said that? It passed right through my thoughts while thinking about how to answer a question he never asked me. Quickly I started flipping through the previous thirty seconds of thoughts like pages in a book to find a vapor trail with words left on it. *Something about the basketball court upstairs...*

"Uh, oh, yeah, basketball court?"

"What are you smoking, Big Man? I said they are getting rid of the basketball court upstairs."

"Oh, yeah, someone else said that too," I recovered. "Stevenson's going to come back and haunt every board member who made that decision. It pisses me off too. They are ditching the court so they can put fancy new aerobic machines in so it will attract younger, more beautiful people."

"We could use some younger, more beautiful people around here," Wilson laughed. Then he got serious again. "What you talking about, bully's and shit?"

"Well you asked me, 'Why they got to do that?' And it got me thinking about why some people beat up on some people, and why some people use their power to keep other people down."

"Man, they been doing that forever. They did it to Jesus, man," Wilson said with authority, as if he had been there.

"You know why they did it to Jesus, Big Man?" Again he looked me in the eyes as if we were lined up opposite one another on the field.

"To save us from our sins," I offered lamely.

"No, man. That's crap. They crushed him 'cause he was stirring up trouble, just like they do you or me. It weren't no Jews and religious higher-ups like they always saying, it was the Romans that killed Jesus. You know what those Romans used to do?"

"No, what?" I was curious.

"I watched it on the History Channel. Those Roman Senators and rich folk bought land on the frontier of their empire, just like they do today. They loaned those peasants money and when they couldn't pay it back with interest, they took the land. Then they made those same peasants dat used to own the land, rent their own land back from 'em.

"I have people down South, farming families, and they've been doing that down there for centuries, for centuries. They still doing it, man – whether it's your house in the city or some skinny ass farmer's land in the country. Jesus didn't sit still for that shit, and he organized those peasants and they started standing up for themselves. Standing up for themselves."

"So Jesus was a Community Organizer?" I asked.

"Something like that. You know what else them Romans did?"

"What?"

"That man, Pontus Pilate, the Roman governor of that place, he once crucified so many people that the dead lined the road on both sides for almost twenty miles. Think about the stink? A feast for vultures and crows! Think about how much wood it took for them crosses? What if you was a peasant watching all them crucifixions? You'd be thinking to yourself, 'If they willing to go to all that trouble to kill us, there ain't nothing they won't do.' So then maybe you give up."

"I see what you mean. State terror. It's kind of like those cops I saw beating up the drunk and challenging me: 'I dare you to start something.' And they have so much more power than you, that you just back away and call it a day."

"Yeah, except Jesus. Except Jesus." Wilson was puffed up bigger than I had ever seen him. It was as if everything he ever knew or cared about was balanced on that one graphic moment in time.

"Jesus faces 'em down." Wilson was at once deadly serious and robust. "He doesn't shout and he doesn't cry. They take him to that elevator in the back of the jailhouse and they beat the shit out of him, and he doesn't say nuthin'. Nothing. It's like he isn't even there and they get spooked, get spooked."

"How's that help anything?"

"Man, it's not about helping something, Big Man, it's about *doing* something." He says it as if I can't add two and two and get the right answer.

"Jesus, he takes the worst they can dish out and never makes a sound. He doesn't flinch. He doesn't groan. He gives 'em nothin'. They whip him with leather that's got little glass beads tied into it. Nothing. They throw salt on his back when they're done. Nothing. They hammer a nail in one hand and then the other. Nothing. They can't make him peep! They hang him up naked. Nothing. Yeah, he's hanging out for the whole world to see and it's as if he doesn't give a shit. Nothing. He's hanging there for hours, maybe days, and the crows come up and pick at him. Beetles crawl in his ear. Mosquitoes suck his blood. Flies lay eggs in the holes in his hands. Nothing. Jesus is saying, by not saying nothing the whole time, 'You got nothing.' He is up in Pilate's face, even though he's hanging on a hill, and he's saying, 'You don't own me and you don't own these people.' And that's the one thing

Pilate can't stand to hear. 'The Man' can't stand to hear *nothing* when he puts a beating on you."

Wilson was staring at me, his eyes drilling holes deep into my soul.

"And that's why, when them sheriffs beat my ass, they got *nothing*. I closed my eyes and I remembered Jesus and I knew that if he could go the distance, I could go the distance with those fat fools. The more quiet I was the angrier they got and the stronger I felt. I'm not a churchgoer but I'll tell you this: Jesus was king that day."

"Wilson," I said looking right back into his root beer brown eyes, "I never, in all my life, heard Jesus told that way. You ought to be a preacher because I like that Jesus a whole lot more than the one I heard about."

"Well, Big Man, you got to be beat down to meet *that* Jesus. Ain't nothing free," he said and started to laugh.

I didn't know whether to laugh or cry, be jealous, or repulsed. Suddenly I was on my side of Main Street looking across the Jordan River. Over on the other side waving at me was Jesus. I stood there but didn't know how to cross and started to feel panicky. Suddenly getting to the other side was the only thing I cared about.

"Next time you see some poor old drunk being beat up by cops, you say something, Big Man. You call out to them cops and tell 'em what they're doing is wrong, and if you do that, you'll meet *that* Jesus!"

He laughed a deep, deep belly guffaw that filled the steam room with a sonic boom. "You do that, Big Man, and you'll be meetin' *that* Jesus."

The door opened and Estefan walked in.

"What are you fellas laughing about?" he asked in the snippy little bank teller way he has.

Wilson's eyes grew big as saucers and as he glared at me, the grin on his face grew and grew as if we knew something Estefan would never know. Then he laughed again and as disturbed as I felt, it infected me. My belly jiggled and rumbled and what began down in the pit of my stomach, shook its way up to my throat and burst out my lips with the force of Jesus on the Third Day. I laughed and cried at the same time, tears and snot rolled down my face and spit flew from my mouth.

The longer Estefan stood there bewildered, the more it fed our laughter. Finally, poor old Estefan shrugged and left. Like a car motor sputters out with too much choke, so did our laughter.

"Peace out, Big Man," Wilson waved as he got up to leave the steam room. "Mmm, mmm, mmm," he said, shaking his head with a chuckle as the door closed behind him.

Chapter Eighteen

Kokomo

I'd never seen Koko in the steam room before.

Kokomo King was a personal trainer, a fixture in the weight room with his red COE Center "Staff" shirt and black pants neat as a pin. He had a loud, resonant baritone laugh that echoed off the bare walls. But there he was in the steam room, head in hands and the gravity of something pushing his elbows into muscular quads. It was the steam room *blues* posture. A guy sitting like that, staring at the floor with his shoulders rolled over has brought the weight of the world into the steam room.

Koko was fully capable of carrying the weight of the world. He was only about six feet tall but the girth of his biceps was greater than most men's waist, and the quadriceps forming his thighs were like two pier pylons strong enough to moor a freighter. He could bench four hundred and ninety-five pounds and still, like so many Paul Bunyan characters, his demeanor was as gentle as it was kind and jovial.

He was a Deacon at the Abyssinian Metro African-Methodist-Episcopal Zion

Church, where at least twenty-five percent of the Eastside population does business, belongs, or visits for weddings and funerals. Koko is the Pied Piper for an archipelago of small groups the church formed for the nurture of young African American males, and he has carried the program to success on the force of his strong and affectionate manner. Seeing him there, stripped from the waist up, leaning into those bear claw hands and glistening in the heat of the steam room, it was impossible to miss the aura of sorrow radiating outward from his heart.

Koko didn't look up when I opened the door and entered, so I did not disturb him – which is a sensitivity protocol that separates men from boys. Instead, I sprayed for steam and watered off the tile ledge before sitting down. I was easy with the silence but at the same time, I didn't want him to think I couldn't see the hurt dripping with sweat from his pores.

"Hey Koko, you look down."

"Yeah," he muttered to the floor through a gap between his palms.

"Want to vent?"

Slowly and just barely, his head raised just enough to look at me and consider the offer. "I got a problem and I don't know what to do about it. *I* don't have the problem," he added, "somebody else does, but I don't know what to do about it."

"I don't know if I can help but I'm a

pretty good listener."

Quiet followed. Looking at Koko I realized this was the first time I'd seen him shirtless. His colossal torso was rippled with muscles in places I'm pretty sure I don't have any. It made me think of those big Belgian draft horses with mountainous muscles bulging from their chests, and small foothills of sinew rippling down their shoulders underneath an extravagance of mane.

How lovely I heard myself think, an exclamation aimed more toward God than myself. It was the same kind of appreciative awe that leaks out when a Great Blue Heron flies over a pond in the pink of dusk.

"Okay," he mumbled. "So I met this little lady in the grocery. And I mean little. She's a Chinese lady but not really a lady, not yet. She looks like she's fourteen years old but she says she's twenty. She can hardly speak English. I mean, she's like, you know, like how they make fun of Asian folk, the way they talk and everything."

"Where did you meet," I asked.

"The grocery, *Tops*, over there on Niagara Street. It's the 'Tops of the World' we call it, 'cause you walk from aisle to aisle and hear every language from every country in the world."

"Yeah," I chuckled, "I go there when I want to make *real* rice and beans."

"She was looking lost," he said, "so I asked if she needed help. I ended up helping the little thing find what she was looking for. Then the next time I was there she was too, still looking lost. So I talked to her and kind a helped her around again."

His tone and demeanor was familiar, and I got the feeling that Koko was about to confess to a love affair. The thought of it made me miserable inside because it would ruin his life.

"Anyway, to make a long story short, after I helped her in the store half a dozen times maybe, I invited her to come home and meet my family. She was real nervous at first and said she really shouldn't. But the next time I asked, she said she would. I had already told my wife about her so she wasn't surprised when I walked in that night with a Chinese lady for dinner."

I gulped when I realized that I had just done to Koko what everybody does to me, which is assume I got defrocked because of an affair.

"She met my kids and they asked her all kinds of questions about China, but she is from Taiwan. My eight-year-old son is as tall as she is so he calls her 'the little adult.' We laughed a lot and answered questions for her about living in the United States. We asked her how she got here and she told us her boyfriend brought her over and when she talked about him, she just glowed with sunshine."

With this image fresh in his memory,

Koko smiled a huge toothy grin and it shifted the mood of the entire room. But it was only for a moment.

"Then, the next time I saw her, she invited me to come over to see her little apartment. So I did. I bought her a little flowering plant at the check-out and gave it to her for the apartment. That made her real happy.

"It's a nice enough apartment," he went on, "but only one room with a bathroom, you know, everything all in one room. She makes it look clean and nice. And then she takes me over to the bookshelf and kind of preens real big as she shows me pictures of her boyfriend, his big face smiling through the shiny glass of framed photos. I know him. He's one of the deacons at my church. I also know his wife and three kids."

A dump truck just pulled up to the steam room, raised its bed, opened the gate, and down comes a ton of shit, splat. Suddenly I felt the heaviness of Koko's dilemma. He is leaning harder than ever into the fulcrum of those elbows and seems even more spent from having told the story.

"Oh man, that's complicated," is all I could think to say.

"Everyone's going to get hurt in this mess and you don't want to be the source of it, right?" I added after I had several seconds to think about it.

"That's right. I don't want it to be my

business but the dude is making it my business. We're looking for a new minister and one of the candidates we interviewed has been divorced. This same deacon is telling everyone on the Board of Deacons that we can't have a divorced preacher – that he wouldn't be a strong moral example for us. Can you believe that shit?"

"Do you think it's true what everyone says, that churches are full of hypocrites?"

"Man, we don't got the corner on hypocrisy. It's just that we aim higher so it looks worse when we fall. But the dude isn't just a hypocrite; he's a low-down snake. He goes to Taiwan for business and he meets this sweet little girl over there, and he has the balls to bring her back as his private Geisha or some shit like that. His kids play with my kids, his wife is a friend with my wife, and we are deacons together. What am I supposed to do?"

"I suppose you would take it to the head minister if you had one, huh?"

"Yeah, that's exactly what I *would* do. I would lay it right down at his feet and tell him not to tell anyone that I was the snitch." Then after a pause he adds, "You know what the worse thing is?"

"What?"

"That sweet little China girl is going to get screwed big time, and I'm not talking sex. What do you think is going to happen to her when the whole thing blows up? He's gonna drop her like a hot coal, and where's she going to go? See what I mean?"

"Yeah, that's ugly."

Then we are both sitting face in hands, feeling the weight of a troubled world on our shoulders. I only knew one of the characters involved but suddenly I felt his grief and sorrow as if it were my own. In the split screen in my head, one half is manacled by the gravity of Koko's situation while the other side is thinking that in its own way, being able to feel someone else's troubles like this is as beautiful as Koko's muscles or a Great Blue Heron. Who made us like this, capable of something so majestic as compassion?

"I dunno, man," I finally broke the silence. "Seems like whichever way you go you got problems. But one thing I do know that might help is a friend that works with refugees, and she could help the young woman when the time comes."

"Thanks, I'll take you up on that." Koko reached over and slapped me a limp five as he left the steam room, those bulbous round shoulders slumped forward like he was still Atlas carrying the world out with him.

My dad had an affair.

It shattered my world because it was at the same time I found out about sex. My next-door neighbor, Tommy Meeks, gave me the news. We were in the fort we built under the bushes between our two houses. It was dark and damp and slightly muddy, no place our older sisters would venture under any circumstances - perfect for hiding out.

Tommy, who was a year ahead of me in school, asked why my dad was having "an affair." He said it with dramatic emphasis, like he'd known the phrase forever even though he had just learned it. When I asked him what an affair was, he told me it was when a man has sex with a woman not his wife. Then I had to ask him what sex was, and he told me it was putting your penis in a girl's hole, and neither one of us knew the word "vagina."

I remember the explosion in my head at the simultaneous entry of those two images: any penis inside another body and my father's penis inside another woman. The image of my mom and dad having sex was ugly enough but my dad doing it with someone else was even more disgusting.

Anger swelled inside until it came gushing out with a punch between Tommy's eyes. He punched me back and we started wrestling so violently that the fort fell down around us. I don't remember exactly how it ended except that both of us ran away at the same time covered in mud and blood.

Tears streaming down my cheeks, I ran into the house, up the back stairs and tripped on the top step, flying full force face down on the second floor hallway. My mother, who was coming out of the bathroom, guffawed at the sight, and then yelled that it served me right for running in the house with mud on my shoes. My anger flashed at her, empowering me to get up in spite of my wounds and I yelled back, "Why didn't you tell me dad had an affair!"

The whitening of her cheeks, the wet saucers of her widened eyes, the bitten lower lip and speechless stare before turning on her heels and running away, is seared in my memory. I had no idea what was happening around me, but on a visceral level I knew my powerful and invulnerable mother had just been lacerated and deeply wounded.

Later I would find out that Tommy had overheard the news from his parents talking about it, and that my dad had been so inept at keeping it secret that it was common knowledge. My mother's response was to retreat into the walls of her house and not appear outside for months, raising the toxicity level in our home exponentially. For his part, my dad became more and more passive, which itself was an astonishing achievement given how passive he was before 'the affair.'

Children never know their parents. We imagine we do but that is fantasy or wishful thinking. By the time children have grown and are old enough to have a relationship of adult mutuality with their parent, the parent has consumed forty, fifty or even sixty years of living that the child has never truly known or can understand. That is an insurmountable distance to bridge, but add to such separation all the intimacies of a married relationship that will never be revealed plus all the projections we vomit on our parents, and the impossibility of comprehension becomes clear.

I felt exhausted and unnerved, the cloud of steam dissipated and the glaring white walls screamed at me from every side. I hoped that deacon's children never found out what their father had done. Then again, I supposed the fact that he could be so duplicitous meant he had probably inflicted all kinds of other pain on them already.

There is so much pain in the world and so many people to pile it on.

Chapter Nineteen

Ichabod Crane

Ted was the spitting image of Ichabod Crane, the long lanky schoolteacher from the Legend of Sleepy Hollow. Galumphing from one foot to the other in an awkward bouncing fashion, wearing only a towel, his gangly arms and short waist made him downright cartoonish. Like the character Ichabod, it was never clear whether he was a victim of his unfortunate appearance – awkward but nice – or if he harbored a much darker personality inside amidst that ungainly exterior.

Take for instance how he relished setting Dweedle off. All of us did it a little, goosing a small burst of expletives to light up the otherwise morose atmosphere in the early morning locker room. But Ted took it to another level.

Ted persistently aggravated Dweedle, poking him until he yelled and carried on so vehemently that the gun holstered in his locker was on everyone's mind. It began when Ted asked who Dweedle was going to vote for, or what he's got against The Clan, or anything to do with an assortment of characters in the local Republican party. Ted knew it would rankle Dweedle's resentment and produce a thunderclap.

"Say, what about that Collin Christie," I heard Ted ask out of the blue one morning, referring to the Republican County Executive who was the nephew of the party boss who sold Dweedle up river. Dweedle burst open with invective and the roaring torrent of bile was so caustic and loud everyone fled the locker room in fear of what might happen.

Ted lighting Dweedle's fuse was the first thing I heard when I walked through the door of the steam room one morning. The F-bombs immediately rained down upon all the inhabitants of the locker room.

The day before had been a "Lake Effect" snowstorm, the kind Buffalo is famous for. Ted knew Dweedle's street was one of the last in the city to be cleared – because in Buffalo grudges can last for decades. I wanted to crouch when I heard Ted ask Dweedle if *they* cleared his street yet.

A lake effect storm takes place when the ice on Lake Erie has not frozen solid and a frigid storm sweeps in from Canada moving from east to west. The winds grab up moisture off the lake and it increases the density of snow manifold degrees. A dark, ominous gathering of clouds appears over the lake and moves into the downtown, or anywhere along the shore, sometimes bringing with it the bad sisters of fog and lightning along with snow falling to the earth in sheets as if it were rain.

Such a band of lake effect snow may be several miles wide or only half a mile, but it dumps with uncanny precision four, five or six feet of snow on one town, one neighborhood, or even one section of a neighborhood. An average winter snowfall in Buffalo is ninety inches or so, and there have been winters when eighty of those inches came in one storm and landed on only one small section of the city.

I moved quickly to the steam room to leave behind the expletive-laced diatribe Ted had sparked. In addition to safety and steam I was delighted to find, "Haarb!"

Haarb Nadjr, possibly the COE's only Muslim member, sat in one corner smiling up at me. The yelling moved into the background immediately subdued by Haarb's infectious grin.

He was a steam room junkie too, but he worked out in the late afternoon or early evening so we didn't see each other much.

Several times a year, when circumstances required one of us to cross the boundary of our routines and exercise at a different time in the day, we ran into each other in the steam room. The first time we met, one afternoon two years ago in the steam room, Haarb's familiar television tagline was spawned. Now everyone in Western New York has a reaction to it, scorn from some and laughter from others. A personal injury and criminal attorney, Haarb was looking for a saucy phrase that would become an earworm in the general public, and that afternoon a steam room cabal produced one: "Caught driving home from the bar? Call Haarb Nadjr!"

Haarb made a sweeping arm motion as if a maître d' showing me to my table, and said he was hiding from the snow in the warmest place he could think of. Just as I sat down in the opposite corner and stretched my legs out on the bench, Hamm walked in.

"Happy Good Friday," Hamm said in a monotone voice as he sat down between us, likely morose at having to restrict himself to a third of the steam room.

"Now there's a paradox if ever there was one," I said, not registering the complexity of emotion I felt over not remembering what day it was. "But Haarb here is Muslim," I added, "so he's not into Good Friday."

"Is that the Christian holiday where everyone puts ashes on their forehead and walks around pretending they don't know there is a smudge there?" Haarb asked.

"That's Ash Wednesday," Hamm offered, again in a monotone voice.

"Hey, Haarb, Muslims don't believe Jesus died on a cross, do they?"

"No, the Koran says that Jesus, blessed be his name, was a great prophet and it would be impossible for one of Allah's rasuls (prophets) to be victimized by such evil. He was taken up by Allah, like Elijah was, and some believe, without ever experiencing death."

Hamm sat up straight, his eyes widened into giant marbles. "You mean Muslims believe in Jesus?"

Haarb and I looked at each other to see who would answer. I offered Haarb the right of way.

"Well, sir, Muslims believe that Jesus was a great prophet, one of the greatest ever. We believe he was born of a virgin birth by his blessed mother, Miriam, and that he came to bring a message to his people, the Jews. However, we do not believe he was, as Christians claim, a son of God because God is One and can have no children. God is one and cannot be three, or two. So, 'yes,' Muslims 'believe' as you say, in Jesus, but we believe something different."

"Huh," Hamm grunted in authentic surprise, then looked at me. "You believe in Jesus, *Surfer Dude*?"

"Hey, only Maggie gets to call me that," I snarled in mock protest. "Do I believe in Jesus?" I echoed back. "Yeah, I believe something about Jesus, I'm just not sure that it is what most Christians believe about Jesus. Why do you ask, *Lucian*?"

"I've seen crucifixion, I know what it's like. I was one of the soldiers that did it."

Silence. The room suddenly felt dark and tight. I could not imagine what the hell Hamm was talking about but whatever it was, it was deadly and serious.

"Good Friday means something different to me than it does to most people," Hamm grimaced. "I can tell you this: you never wash the blood off your hands."

Haarb and I looked at each other again, as if through Hamm who sat between us. Haarb gave me a look like, "You know this guy?" I looked back with seriously diminished confidence that said, yes I do. At that moment, the way he looked and what he sounded like, it would be easy to peg Hamm for a delusional whacko. Then he seemed to wake up, his whole body shuddering for a microsecond.

"I'm not making stuff up. I know it sounds nuts, and I guess I am a little bit, but with good cause. Really, I'm not crazy. It's just that ..." he trailed off again before coming right back. "It's just that I've seen stuff. I've done stuff. And on Good Friday it haunts me worse than other days. On Good Friday a cloud of darkness wraps me up head first in a turban of grief."

Hamm was speaking in a tone of voice I had never heard from him before. It was resonant and clear, a bit halting in its gait but not at all shy or hesitant. He looked back and forth at each of us, both eyes watery with emotion yet crystal clear.

Then he looked away from us, straight

183

ahead into the glass door of the steam room. But he was staring into the glass as if into another dimension. Now it appeared as if Hamm could see in the glass the scene unfold that he began to narrate.

"The Atlacatl Battalion was in no mood to show mercy," he began mid-thought as if we knew what he was talking about. Then, without looking at us, still watching the scene as it appeared to him in the glass reflection, he seemed to intuit our confusion because he added, "Atlacatl was the most elite unit of the Salvadoran Army. They were trained, equipped and attended by a select unit of the United States Special Forces. I know, because I trained them."

With this Hamm spoke in a military cadence: staccato, definite, and precise.

"It was December 10th, 1981 at 5:30 PM when the Atlacatl Battalion entered the village of El Mozote. They separated the two hundred peasant-farmers of that dusty, dog-eared village of Evangelical Christians who, we learned later were staunchly anti-communist, into four groups: men, young women, old women and children. They locked each group into separate buildings as we watched.

"The next day, the young women were taken into the hills and raped before being shot. The men were tortured to extract information then shot, some of them beheaded with machetes. The old women were tortured then shot. The children were likewise killed;

some of them hung, some shot, some beheaded."

"They got sloppy though," he said with a note of irony. "A seven year old boy survived by hiding in the bushes. He watched from his hiding place and told a United Nations Commission."

Haarb and I were frozen in the cloud of steam that hung in the room and descended from swirls buffeting the ceiling. I noticed my mouth gaping open and saw Haarb's opened too.

This was not the kind of confession you ever expected to hear, especially not at eight in the morning in the steam room. Hamm reported it, line after line, as if reading an efficient officer's Duty Log.

I felt the panic inside of wanting to run out of the steam room in horror that Hamm stood by and watched a massacre, *someone I knew*. Yet I wanted to put my arms around him and tell him it would be all right. And I wanted to puke. I wanted to scream. I wanted to cry. But I was frozen between repulsion and compassion and couldn't move. I looked at Haarb whose chest wasn't moving in and out.

Then Hamm began again, as if reading from another report, this one also projected in the glass door.

"On May 14, 1990, three hundred non-combatant villagers from Las Aradas fled bombardment by Unit 1 of the Salvadoran National Guard and sought to escape across the Sumpul River on which the little farming hamlet was located. Directly across the river was Honduras and safety. But as the villagers crossed the river the Honduran Army, who we armed and trained, appeared silently on the bluff above the river and blocked their escape. I was there, completing the end of my third tour of duty, nearly a decade of training Latin Americans in counter insurgency."

We watched Hamm's eyes survey the scene all over again, as if he had watched the scene unfold a thousand times, and knew exactly how each body twisted and turned as it fell.

"The Salvadoran Army unit behind the villagers opened fire. All three hundred were massacred. In the Truth Commission hearings that followed the war, one old woman told about losing fifty of her family members on that one day at the Sumpul River."

Hamm fell silent.

Haarb and I sat absolutely still. My thoughts were as frozen as my body. Nothing. The steam was gone. The florescent white light fluttered ever so slightly and emitted a small whine. The tile seemed whiter yet filthier than ever. The only other sound was issued by drips from the ceiling. Whatever happened to Dweedle was ancient history and the world outside disappeared behind the walls of that moment, in that room, and held only the three of us.

"Jesus was *no different* than those poor

bastards, or the ones we tortured after 9/11," Hamm said, breaking the silence.

"I have seen your Good Friday enactments on television," Haarb's voice was gentle and quiet, almost reverent, as if speaking gently to an angry dog on the sidewalk. "I think maybe you make a good point. Instead of dramatizing the ancient story of Jesus being executed, it might be better to see and hear *our victims* ... and acknowledge *ourselves* as agents of brutality."

I looked hard at Haarb.

Is that what Hamm was saying? I didn't hear it that way if he did. Suddenly my thoughts became unfrozen, flocking into a tangled mass of intersecting streams.

Maybe it was dishonest to drape our churches in black, make sad faces, and tell the Passion story in somber tones as if Jesus' torture and death was somehow sadder, worse, or more tragic than all the other tortures and massacres, then or now. Surely Jesus, of all people, I heard myself say, would not see his own torture and death as any different than any other, before or after?

Hamm said what had just dawned on me for the first time in my half-century of life.

"*We* are the Romans," he said it so clearly that it harmonized with my simultaneous thought. "We are the Romans in the story of Jesus," he said again, as if telling himself to listen. Then he fell silent.

Suddenly everything was all so clear:

Christians have told The Passion story for centuries as if *they* were the victims – vicarious victims via Jesus' torture and execution. All the church-talk makes it seem as if a handful of first century Jews were the oppressor. But there I was sitting next to Haarb, a Muslim, and Hamm, a soldier, and suddenly it hit me that the Jews of Jesus' day were Iraqi villagers under United States occupation then. The Jews of Jesus' day were Afghani farmers who once were occupied by the Ottomans, then by the British, then by the Soviets, and now by the United States. The Jews of Jesus' day were Salvadoran villagers rounded up and massacred.

Jesus and his fellow Jews were not like us, we who live inside the privilege of our super economic empire. The Jews were not the Church, with its imperial structure and colonial history, its bishops and clergy enmeshed with the institutions of power. Jesus and his followers, along with his contemporary enemies, were victims of an occupying army. My thoughts were racing down a road they had never been before.

"We are the Roman citizens in the Jesus story," Hamm said for a third time. "We are sitting here and don't even know Jesus is being crucified. Just like the Romans in Jesus' day, we are back home safe and sound in our beautiful churches, and sitting around our sumptuous tables, and fretting about how many points the market lost while, right now, somewhere within the tentacles of our empire, Jesus is being tortured. Somewhere, and probably in many places at *our* behest, and paid for with *our* money, and committed in *our* name, just like the Romans in Jesus' day, a Jesus or two or three is being killed."

Out of the corner of my eye I caught the image of Ted passing by outside the steam room on his way to the shower, and once again I could hear Dweedle shouting invectives in the background.

I got up, leaving Hamm and Haarb sitting there in silence while I left to see if I could calm Dweedle down.

Chapter Twenty

Simulated Running

In my dream I was running.

It was one of those dreams that weaves itself through wakefulness and sleep almost all night long. In it I ran with the wind. But in the gravity of reality I have a total absence of cartilage in one knee and precious little left in the other, running is purely a fantasy or dream for me.

All the more delicious that in my dream I was running effortlessly, and so fast that I outran two Dobermans chasing me. It was night in my dream with the dome of the sky blackened but thick with stars. I ran with abandon on a dewy golf course somewhere, just for fun. No one was stirring anywhere and it felt wonderful to be all alone running. It was almost weightlessness, just running in the night. Then the dogs appeared out of a glade between two arboretums. I didn't know whose they were but I could tell they were gunning for me. Just as one was about to take a bite out of my ass I turned up the burners and left them in a silent wake. It was magical and I didn't want to wake up.

The new elliptical machines The COE

bought with its six million-dollar renovation campaign must have inspired my dream. Dozens and dozens of new machines simulating human activity from lifting to running were suddenly lining the workout space. Looking at them lining the rooms still wrapped in plastic, it slapped me in the face that people pay money to go to a gym, sweat, and do grueling exercises they don't really want to do, all because our lives are so void of strenuous activity that we would otherwise melt into a puddle of amino acids or puff up like a blowfish.

Yet it was one of those new machines that was the source of my all night running ecstasy. While the construction crew was on lunch break, Maggie snuck me into the new part of the facility to show off the amazing array of spectacular equipment. She was so proud and wanted me to see the gleaming bounty of the new wing because I had been grousing ceaselessly about the renovation.

"Go ahead, try one," she giggled like a schoolgirl.

"But it doesn't open until next week," I snorted, a bit uncomfortable with the idea of picking out one machine among sixty or seventy and being the only one exercising in the huge room that used to be a basketball gymnasium – my basketball court. The place where just a few weeks ago our cadre of guys and one woman played ball every Monday, Wednesday, and Friday at noon, and the only place I actually ran any more, was now a freshly painted, partially carpeted Mecca of health. Shortly, scores of people would be imitating natural human activity on those machines and with weights. But standing there I had to admit, in spite of my many objections to the renovation, they had created an aesthetically pleasing space with a mind-boggling array of choices.

"Oh come on, be the first," she gushed.

"Okay, but if I get in trouble you're going down with me. After the Gina and Rebecca escapade they may not be so forgiving."

Maggie trotted back to the main desk and closed the door to that secret garden yet to be discovered by the rest of the world. I climbed up on one of the few unwrapped machines that said it was both elliptical and step at the same time. Indeed, it sported handles that moved with your arms so you could move them just as if actually running. Awkwardly discovering through trial and error how to move precisely in the way the machine wanted me to move, eventually it became smooth and kinetically pleasing.

Lights flashed all manner of numbers telling me how fast I was going, how far I had gone, and how many calories I was burning. The machine imitated running with eerie accuracy and suddenly I was moving at full throttle, something I had not done in years.

The machine measured my stride and indicated with an orange light when my arms and legs were moving in the optimal range of motion. Even at this speed and sweating profusely, I could not feel the weight of my body on either knee or hips. It felt miraculous. For thirty minutes, until the workmen started reappearing, I ran as if the wind were truly in my face. It was disconcerting that a machine allowed me to run again and I felt torn by excitement and resentment. That night, in my dream, I ran with the dogs.

In the afterglow of my dream the next morning, and feeling grateful to Maggie, I wanted to remember to tell her about the dream on the way in. But I couldn't because Mansa was leaning on the front desk talking to her.

Mansa was one of the gym rats who talked as much as she exercised. She had a workout partner named Fabian she lifted weights with, a spinning partner named Gloria, and a floor exercise pal named Wu Lin.

Even before I open the first of the two glass doors at the entryway to The COE, I could hear Mansa's exaggerated voice. She told Maggie that Fabian flipped her on the butt with a towel so hard it formed a welt that was still there two days later. Then, looking right at Maggie, and in a faux whisper I could hear as I opened the second door, she conceded she liked it. When Mansa saw me she grinned even bigger, and confessed that every time it throbbed she got a buzz. Maggie's pale white skin was splotchy pink all the way to her scalp.

"Want one on the other side?" I asked passing the desk on my way downstairs.

Now Mansa blushed ever so slightly and giggled. Maggie rolled her eyes.

"Thanks for yesterday, Maggie, it was great!" I said passing through the turnstile. As I looked back over my shoulder I could see Maggie glowing in the warmth of my slight affirmation and Mansa smirking at the double entendre.

The locker room was quiet, only Dweedle sitting on the bench reading the paper. I did not feel very social anyway so getting into my gym clothes in silence and wandering upstairs to the temporary weight room we had to use during the construction phase suited me just fine. The only person lifting weights that morning in the awkward, crowded chaos of benches, barbells and weight machines was Alvarez. I nodded at him.

Alvarez was just sitting there on a padded exercise bench, a thirty-five pound hand weight next to each of his feet and a seventy-pound barbell on the floor in front of him. He nodded back and muttered an indistinguishable salutation.

"What's up, Alvarez?" I forced myself to be friendly.

"I'm getting married, dude, in two days."

"Married? I didn't know that, congratulations. Hey, you're supposed to be excited."

"Right. How you gonna be excited, man, with everyone telling you you're making a mistake?"

I looked at him sitting there all shriveled up in a pitiful lump and his youthfulness almost shined like a beacon. I saw Alvarez at least four days a week and we bantered now and again. But looking over at him it suddenly hit me how utterly familiar he seemed even though truly, he was a stranger to me.

A wave of remorse or shame buffeted me, although honestly, I am never sure which is which. After two years of lifting weights in the presence of Alvarez, I'm not sure I ever really *looked* at him before. I mean, I had looked at him but maybe never really *seen* him.

His tattoo of Mick Jagger's lips was partially covered by the thin strap of his sleeveless undershirt, and while I knew the tattoo was there, I had never really looked at his face, hands or legs. The dissonance of his sour mood and the advent of his wedding woke me up and I saw him for the first time.

I was struck by how young his face looked: the skin so taut, smooth, and fresh. His youthfulness was sullied only by stringy black hair falling down around his cheeks to frame his face, and a wispy Fu Manchu mustache curved downward around the corners of his lips, nearly meeting in the middle of his chin. A third wisp of hair hung in a Custer-style goatee dripping like Spanish moss from underneath the pronounced curvature of his bottom lip. Alvarez's raggedy appearance successfully screened attention away from his tender age but then if I had ever really looked at him, I could have seen he was in his late teens or early twenties.

"Are they saying it's a mistake because of who you're marrying or is it just all that shit men say about, 'Last chance for freedom' and crap like that?"

"Not her, man, but getting hitched. You know, like no one says they're happy for me. It's like I got a cancer or somethin'. I'm just wondering, maybe I'm making a mistake. Like I looked at her last night, her little face asleep on the pillow and drooling, and thought to myself, *this is it, man, forever. Just her.*"

"It's the 'forever' thing that's got you spooked. It's because there is nothing else in your life that you say 'Yes' to forever."

"Dude, *forever*. Like that is the only nooky you're ever gonna get, ever again. Like *ever*. Like the judge looking down and telling you, 'Life'."

"If you think nooky is the most important part of the deal, maybe you better think about calling it off."

"Huh? What do you mean, man?"

"I mean having sex with only one woman is not the hardest part of marriage."

"No? What's harder than that?"

"Fighting. Fighting over little shit and sticking with it until you get it figured out and you are both happy. All the little shit like putting the toilet seat down, whether you squeeze the toothpaste in the middle or at the end, how you fold laundry - *whether* you fold laundry. I mean all that little stuff there is to fight about. If you don't solve the little stuff it'll all back up like sludge in the pipes and you won't be able to take on the really big stuff - like how often you're going to have sex."

"Everyone says 'don't sweat the little stuff' but you're saying to sweat it, man?"

"Yeah, that's right. If you don't sweat the little stuff it'll get stuck in your craw like a seed between your teeth. It'll just sit there and fester every time it happens again, and there will be lots of those little things that will get stuck. And they'll pile up, and then to get into one will be to get into all of them, so then you won't get into anything. When that happens, you've got no future."

Alvarez deflated before my eyes. I could see him melting right there on the bench.

"I don't like arguing, man. She's tougher than me."

"It's always like that. One person is always better at combat than the other one, so you have to find a way to even it out, or you've got no incentive to keep trying."

"But what about the sex, man?" Alvarez asked plaintively.

"Well, actually, that gets better over time. If you think you have good sex now, wait fifteen years when you know each other's body inside and out! The more you know each other the better the sex can be. But it's like everything else, you have to work at it."

I didn't seem to be filling him with confidence. In fact, his golden skin was looking grayish.

"Look," I said, giving up on any chance of solitude with a big sigh and sitting down cross-legged on the floor right in front of him so that I was looking up at his face. "Did you ever get anything out of date-sex and one night stands?"

Alvarez sat up at the thought and momentarily filled his lungs with air and possibilities. "Dude, you're asking 'The Man' if he had good times with women? Hell yes."

"Don't give me that shit, Alvarez," I said knowingly. "You had some good sex and some bad sex, just like everyone else. But there was no sex that ever took away the fact that you are all alone. You ended up lonely in the morning no matter how many times you did it the night before. It's not about sex and it never was. You just thought it was."

He looked at me with a mix of incredulity and puzzlement, like a puppy that wasn't sure what its master wants. But even though his face was twisted up and his head tilted in an overly dramatic gesture of confusion, I could read in his eyes a flash of recognition.

"Whatthefuckareyoutalkingabout, man?" It came out as one multisyllabic word.

"It's about the relationship. It's about going to sleep with someone you know wants to be with you and waking up next to the someone you want to be with. It's about being with someone who knows you so well that she can tell when you are hurt or afraid – even when you are trying to cover it up. It's about being able to put your head on her chest and cry, even as she can let you hold her when she is upset. It is about the *desire* to grow into one another even though, sitting where you are sitting right now, you don't know how or if you can do it."

Alvarez was quiet again but the macho haze disappeared.

He was holding what I said to measure it, to see how solid it was. An invisible verve seemed to be restoring his posture and repairing the lethargic slump into which he had fallen. Even though he wasn't talking I could almost hear the conversation inside his head. Then, suddenly and seemingly apropos of nothing, he started talking.

"There's this old couple in my neighborhood, Dr. and Mrs. Cruz. I've known them as long as I can remember. He's retired now but he was our dentist when we were kids." Alvarez was dreamy, as if strolling down a tunnel of pleasant memories.

"They walk down the street holding hands. You see 'em on their porch or in the grocery staying real close to each other. He's out working on the house and she's bringing him lemonade. She's out sweeping the porch and he's bringing her the dustpan. You can't tell who's taking care of who because they got each other's back all the time. One day I want to be like them, just like old Dr. and Mrs. Cruz."

"That's it!" I proclaimed. "Now you got it. Sex is only one of the colors streaking through that great big painting. If you can imagine it, and if you desire it, and the two of you keep chasing it, then you can have it."

Alvarez shook his head gently, looked at the floor as if there was something going on down there to see. I got up with an old man's grunt, patted him very slightly on the shoulder as I walked past and said, "Marriage is hard work, but it can be the best hard work you'll ever do."

I sat down on a bench at the Smith machine and thought about how much weight I felt like pushing, but underneath conjuring pounds of steel were the echoes of my pep talk to Alvarez. They pulled me deep down into memories and uncertainty. Regrets hung there like broken spider webs. Everything I told Alvarez I learned from failure, my ex-wife and kids suffering as I stumbled into maturity. Maybe, just maybe, I have mined those failures enough to make a go of my current relationship. I took a sip from that half-full glass and escaped those thoughts while the getting was good.

Plopping my water bottle, iPod, and

sweat rag down on the floor next to me, I got up and placed a forty-five pound steel donut on each side. Then came the best part; lying down. I lay down on the bench, scooted myself this way and that to make sure I was exactly in the middle. One bare hand wrapped around the textured metal bar, then the other hand, pushing up just a little to feel if my hands were truly shoulder width apart. I heaved upward: one ... two ... three. My chest filled with air each push up, and deflated as the weight came down balanced on my hands. Four ... five ... six.

A warm burning sensation moved like lava into the muscles in my chest and shoulders. Seven ... eight ... nine: I thought about the sensation of running – freedom and unfettered motion. Ten ... eleven ... twelve: I never really liked to run but losing the ability to run was a grief that dug its deep cellar into my thoughts. Thirteen ... fourteen ... fifteen.

Bringing the bar half way down, I placed it in the clips on either side. Then, rolling out from under the bar, I popped up and pulled a small ten-pound disc off the rack and placed it over the larger forty-five pound plate. Finally I lay down on my back. I started all over again, one ... two ... three. With each motion an inhale or exhale, muscles tightened then stretched, first up then out.

In the dark behind closed eyes I felt that murky pool of grief that's been left unattended. *Why bother with this shit? I'm never going to run again. Hell, I betcha I don't even play real basketball again. It's downhill from here dude, get used to it.* I shake my head to dislodge the thoughts. Eight … nine … ten … eleven: *Never say never. I can run the court a little, knock bodies around in the paint, grab rebounds and on the very best of days, maybe even dunk for the fun of it.*

I added a little five-pound donut to each side, lay back down, clasped my fingers around the bar and heaved upward. A bead of sweat rolled down my forehead, curled around the bridge of my nose and ran into the socket of my eye igniting a new burn. One … two … three: *running is freedom.* Four … five … six: *grief is a weight that pulls you down. Don't go there.* Seven … eight … nine: *but running means you can get away from the grief, leave gravity.* Ten … eleven … twelve: *if I feel the grief I'm acknowledging the loss and that might mean I never run again; never jump, or slide my feet from side to side with tenacious defense.* Thirteen … fourteen … fifteen: the bar landed with a clang above my head.

Sweat dripped down my face like rain so I reached for my rag and wiped my head the way you would clean a bowling ball. I heard Alvarez grunting a count under his breath as he lifted weights ten feet away. I must have zoned out because all of a sudden Alvarez pierced my airspace and woke me up.

"Thanks man. I feel better. I'm getting

married and it's cool."

"It's good," I smiled.

Chapter Twenty-one

The Appeal of Breasts

"I knew a guy who dated an exceptionally unattractive woman for the better part of a year just because she had incredible tits." Frodo smirked with a crooked half smile.

"It was you! Admit it, man, it was YOU," Wilson shouted. We all stared back at Frodo waiting out the pregnant pause. He blushed like red wine on white carpet. The silence was shattered with boisterous laughter rattling the steam room.

"Admit it, everyone has been led by a pair of breasts the way a puppy follows the promise of milk," I chortled.

Wilson stepped out front.

"One time I left my girlfriend at a bar because some wench was shaking her titties at me all night from the other end of the bar, and on the dance floor too. I just followed her out the door when my girlfriend went to the bathroom. That's all, just followed that rack right out the door and never even thought about my girlfriend till it was too late."

Roaring guffaws showered Wilson who shook his head in mock remorse, and every other head wagged up and down like bobbleheads on a dashboard.

Hamm threw his story in the ring.

"I pursued a Delilah in our office for over a year just because of her hellacious Sweater Kittens. She was a bitch really. You know, warm and sweet one minute and cold as ice the next. It took months of buying her little things, leaving anonymous cards and flowers she knew were from me, all of it just to get her to go out with me once. The whole time, all I was interested in were those goddamn chesticles!"

Another wave of laughter rolled over us as we huffed and puffed for breath because Hamm had an endless string of synonyms for those simple mammary. Hamm had to finally elbow his way through the noise of hilarity in order to finish the story.

"So finally, seriously, after like ten months of trying, she goes out with me but only because I got tickets to a Smashmouth concert and promised her good food afterward. We got drunk and went to her place and Jesus Christ, when she pulled off her sweater you could have floated a barge with the padding in her bra. No shit. I've seen fried eggs bigger than those norks. You know what I'm saying? Little tiny tater tots disguised as airbags!"

The steam room rattled with the loudest hoots and snorts yet just as the door opened and Ted and Dweedle poked their faces in.

"What's going on in here," Dweedle

barked with the authority of age contradicted by a twinkle of recognition in his eyes at the familiar sounds of boyish solidarity. Both entered the steam room forcing the rest of us to move closer as coughs and wheezing syncopated the uneven fading laughter.

Wiping tears from my eyes allowed me to see glistening tracks on everyone's cheeks. It is not so much what Hamm said as the scowling way he said it. An unwritten protocol of male story telling about breasts draws on a library of common memory. There aren't even any words in this library, only primitive carnal archetypes that never need to be mentioned while seeding any story with humor. Whether gruff and emotionless or effeminate and silly, male breast-discourse is so primordial that it has its own universal language of tone.

"I dated a nurse once," Estefan peeped and everyone turned in mass astonishment at the sound.

"Was she a wild ride, 'Fan," Wilson hooted.

"Well, yes, she really was," he said with thoughtful earnestness that made us laugh all the more uproariously. "Each of her breasts was bigger than my head," he declared with eyes so wide we laughed even louder. "I really liked them; they were so soft and warm to sleep with. But she was a little strange. She kept dressing me up in different outfits before we made love."

Shockwaves shattered my eardrums as

everyone bent over in hysterics.

"I couldn't do it any more after she made me wear Lederhosen and called me *Johannes* with puckered lips in an Austrian accent."

It became physically painful. It took us several minutes to recover and when we finally did Estefan concluded, "But I missed those breasts for the longest time."

"I knew a woman once," Dweedle jumped in calling on his seniority, "whose boobs leapt from her chest like two sausages on springs, one looking off to the left and the other to the right. The nipples were like one of those paintings with eyes that seem to follow you all around a room. No matter which way you moved," he scowled, "one of her nipples was always looking at you."

Dweedle's aged reflection spawned a new round of laughter and snorting, but it also added recognition that it was not a mere dalliance of middle age or adolescence we had descended into, but an ageless strand of DNA in the male narrative.

"I guess it's true what they say," Koko inserted, "'Women with big tits aren't stupid, big tits make *men* stupid.'" Then he added, "Before I got married all a woman had to do was jiggle those things at me and I was her newest best friend. But since I had kids, and since I seen what they is really supposed to be used for, they lost a lot of charm."

"Ain't that the truth," Frodo assented, a look of mild disgust washing over his face and contorting his mouth.

"Nah, not me," Wilson argued. "It don't make no difference how many babies sucked on those things, they still look fine to me."

The tone of conversation turned philosophical.

"What difference does it make," Dweedle asked, "if they were milked in the past? They all start sagging sooner or later just like *we* all shrink up sooner or later."

That note of reality stung the room into sobriety as audible shudders filled the air.

The mental image of old breasts and shrinking penises scattered the crowd and soon the steam room was down to Wilson and me. A halo of humor hung over us and the pipes clanked as vapor filled the air again. Random chuckles escaped from both of us littering the silence.

"I don't want to freak you out, Wilson," I said after a while, "but did you ever think of God as a woman?" I could see through the fog that he squinted at me from across the room.

"Big Man, I don't think about God much at all," he said flatly, "and I sure don't think of God as no woman. Why you ask?"

"I dunno, I was thinking about breasts, I guess."

"If God has breasts, I'll be thinking about her a lot more," Wilson chuckled.

"Never mind," I retreated, regretting I ventured in that direction.

What got me thinking about it was the

sudden appearance in my thoughts of the random, floating image of Michelangelo's painting of *God creating Adam* splashed across the ceiling of the Sistine Chapel. What if Michelangelo had painted Adam's crooked finger reaching out to touch the nipple of God's female breast extending gracefully toward him, instead of the two males reaching their fingers across the abyss between them? It might have changed everything about Western Civilization. I considered the possibility of discussing this with Wilson then thought better of it.

But I couldn't stop thinking about it.

There are so many sensual ancient Sufi love poems to God. Rabia of Basra imagining God as her lover, Rumi or Kabir yearning to be kissed by God. And the verse from the Song of Solomon I memorized the night before my wedding:

"How fair and pleasant you are,
O loved one, delectable
maiden!
You are stately as a palm tree,
and your breasts are like its
clusters,
I say I will climb the palm tree
and lay hold of its branches.
O may your breasts be like
clusters of the vine,
and the scent of your breath like
apples,

and your kisses like the best wine
that goes down smoothly,
gliding over lips and teeth..."[3]

I looked over at Wilson leaning against the wall in a peaceful repose and opened my mouth to recite this unexpected text of the Bible, but stopped mid-breath. The notion that God was a cosmic woman or that spirituality and sexuality are entangled as if lithe naked bodies in the night, just seemed more than Wilson would want to think about at the moment. Instead I closed my eyes and kept it to myself.

---

[3] Song of Solomon 7:6-9

Chapter Twenty-two

The Tyranny of a Dream

He was a study in sorrow, a human statue frozen in grief. It is difficult to know what or whether to say anything to someone sitting alone in the steam room and clothed in such obvious weariness.

I recognized him from the weight room, a fellow pilgrim on the road to middle age. Upstairs he was always impeccably dressed in fresh clean workout clothes, a perfect advertisement for Nike, Columbia and Puma. Naked under the glaring florescence and ignobly dripped upon by ceiling sweat, he appeared remarkably ordinary, frail even.

In a quiet voice I asked if he minded my turning up the steam. He shook his head okay, then asked me if, when I was a kid, I knew what I wanted to be when I grew up. I told him no, that I never really chased a dream. Then I sprayed the thermostat.

He told me his entire childhood, as far back as he could remember, was filled with dreams and fantasies of becoming a doctor. One Christmas, he recalled, when he was only four or five years old, he received a medical kit. It was a real leather doctor's bag, worn soft and creased with age. In it was a stethoscope, rolls of gauze bandages, a thermometer and dozens of medicine bottles filled with little Pez-like candies. His mom and dad had gone to great lengths to fulfill his Christmas wish of finding him a little white doctor's coat and blue scrubs that would fit. He remembered it fondly as his best Christmas ever.

His dream never changed or veered off path growing up, he told me with dire seriousness. He played sports and did other things but always his eye remained on the goal of becoming a doctor.

For a moment he flashed philosophical while wondering where the seed was planted but he couldn't remember a time without the desire.

In high school Science Club, before there was PETA he noted, he and a buddy performed surgery on a giant white rabbit. After reading extensively about anesthesia, surgical procedures and anatomy, they conducted surgery to remove a tumor from the bunny's neck, keeping their wits about them even when they nicked the artery and a geyser of blood spewed across the room.

The tumor was successfully removed, but the sutured muscles and tissue they sliced to get into the tumor wasn't put back together just right. Afterward they discovered their experiment left the rabbit's head permanently bent to the right. The poor bunny hopped around with its ears pointed to the side.

College was more of the same, where he excelled at chemistry when lesser candidates had to bail. The memory seemed to reinvigorate him a little as his shoulders rose and he spoke with more confidence. Never once, in all four years of undergraduate studies, did he earn less than an A, except in an art history class he had to drop in order to avoid a B. He was admitted to his three top choices for medical school and accepted entrance to Harvard, of course.

At Harvard he did well, in the top third of his class but not the very best as he had been used to achieving. Spurred on by his struggle to be the best among the best, he worked even harder so that he might be accepted to a prestigious residency. But, and then his body slumped again, all of that seemed long ago.

These days, looking back, he stuttered over where the damn dream had come from.

He never enjoyed being a doctor once the goal was met. The fact it had been such a clear and present dream haunted him. Impatiently he began insisting to know where the dream came from.

It was rare that he enjoyed the company of other physicians, he quipped, and the actual business of his craft – intertwined as it was with insurance companies, hospital administration, pharmaceutical pimps, attorneys and government regulation – was a miserable routine of narrow self-interests and conflicting loyalties.

His interactions with patients were a blur of truncated conversation spiked with technological data and information, and consultations with nurse practitioners and specialists, all of whom seemed to know more about the patient than he did.

Whatever he imagined as a child and adolescent about being a doctor, there was little about the profession that truly suited him, he had come to realize. Every day he woke with angst about having to traverse another day through the hospital, and at night he sunk into his chair in depression at having endured another day.

He told me all of this in a spooky voice devoid of light or energy. As he sat in his corner of the steam room talking about the tyranny of a dream, it was with the same passionless droll as reading a weather report from the back page of the newspaper.

As usual, I had two tracks playing in my head. The first was listening to the physician who clearly lived the wrong life and deserved every bit of compassion he evoked. The second track was laced with anxiety, as in, *what the hell am I supposed to say to this guy?*

I started thinking about Doug Proust.

Doug was a high school classmate who knew way back in childhood he wanted to be a doctor. A good looking kid, whose father bought him a shiny new red convertible for his sixteenth birthday. He even acted like a doctor in those days. Doug always had a beautiful girlfriend and was the envy of every guy.

Even though I barely made it out of biology with a C it would never have occurred to me to seek Doug's help, nor was he the kind of a guy to offer. He was a proficient consumer of goods and opportunities, a top feeder in the food chain of success. Yet he aspired to a profession that is supposed to care for people when they are vulnerable and need TLC.

I thought about Doug as I listened to the guy slumped on the bench in the steam room, and I felt the bitter irony of the oxymoron so many physicians seemed to embody: caregiving without the care.

Sitting there in the presence of this man's pain the image of Doug made me shiver even while enveloped in steam. The image of what Doug must have looked like appeared in my head, his white coat pressed and clean and a stethoscope still curled around his neck just below the blue hospital robe he'd used to hang himself with from the eighth floor balcony of his Medical Director's office.

"Have you ever thought of doing something else?" I asked quickly, to erase the image of Doug as much as to show I was listening.

He chuckled ruefully. "I can't afford to."

It was said so flatly and without follow up that I felt it was a stupid question. Then he added, "My wife and kids, and my first wife for that matter, all demand a certain level of income. I have two homes, kids beginning college, an office and partners, a retirement fund ..."

With each sacrament of expense his voice became more weighted until finally it flattened into silence altogether. "Besides, what would I do," he whispered ruefully.

"Go back to school and get an A in Art History!"

We both laughed quietly.

It seemed as if there was nothing I could say that would make a difference. He was lodged in the perfect trap: making copious amounts of money, held in high esteem by all, and performing a function both needed and cherished, and yet he was unfulfilled, burdened even. While his talents and nascent abilities were well suited for his profession it did not spark or hold his passion. *What was his passion?* I almost wondered this out loud but bit my tongue.

"Is there anything you feel passionate about?" I blurted out instead.

"Worms" he chuckled.

"Worms?"

"You know, Earthworms."

"Those fat juicy wrigglers you fish with?"

"Yep. Worms."

That silenced me. I waited to hear more about how someone could be passionate about worms. I waited then couldn't stand it anymore.

"Okay, why worms," I pleaded.

"Did you ever read Charles Darwin?" he asked nonchalantly.

"You mean the Evolution guy?"

"Yes, the 'Evolution Guy,'" he said with a slightly snarky edge to his voice. "He also studied worms. In fact, from the time he returned from his voyage on The Beagle until he died, worms were his passion. That is over forty years' worth."

"And you know this how?" I was incredulous.

"I read his seminal study on worms. He completed it within a year of his death. *The Formation of Vegetable Mould, Through the Action of Worms, with Observations on their Habits.*' Like everything else, Darwin was fascinated by worms and wanted to understand what they did and why."

"Worms?" I said to confirm we really were talking about earthworms.

"Yes, worms. They are captivating. Darwin experimented with music to see if they react to sound, sound quality, or vibration. He played the tin whistle, bassoon and piano, observing their behavior in relationship to which notes were played. He yelled at them to see if they were sensitive to voice or emotion. He even recruited his children to help with the experimentation."

"And my girlfriend thinks I'm eccentric!"

"Perhaps he was eccentric, but you know,

it is people like Darwin that move us forward as a species." He paused for half a minute seeming to catalogue to himself all the great thinkers he admired.

"I do find worms interesting but they are not what I am passionate about. I am passionate about learning. Like Darwin, I am an avid observer of life and a student of the ordinary. I thirst for knowledge. I long to have the time to truly look, to see, to know and understand what others pass by every day. I feel cheated every day that I'm required to hurry through the hours, which is nearly every day. I *hate* it."

His voice turned vociferous, not loud but resonating with bitterness.

"Sounds like you're onto something," I said.

"You're right! I do not want to be on the conveyor everyone else seems so content to be on. I am sick and tired of feeling like a scoundrel and a thief, which is what the insurance and pharmaceutical companies have done to medicine. I am bored to tears with boards and charities that operate at ten thousand feet when what I care most about is minimally at ground level and often subterranean. I am too old and have come too far to put up with pleasantries and cordialities that only mask corruption and petty turf battles. I want out. You're right, I *am* onto something here."

With that he sat up straight and crossed

his arms for emphasis.

I watched him across the way through the veil of vapor and thought he looked regal, like a lion surveying his pride and savannah kingdom. He was suddenly clear and confident and I could almost see his brain at work with tumblers falling inside the lock, opening the path to the bolt. His course of action fell into place right there in the steam room. The man's life was about to change.

The doctor got up, nodded at me, and left.

He left me thinking about dreams and ambitions and the whisper of God along the path of our lives. A minister colleague I know refused to say he had a "calling" because he didn't believe God issues invitations to some people and not to others. Instead he talked about "God's best dream for us." He said that God has a best dream for us as individuals, just like God has a best dream for us as a species. When we are in the groove of that dream, he said, we feel it and everything seems to pop. It is like riding the current of a river rather than swimming upstream or slowly drifting without direction.

Estefan opened the door and I saw that little blue razor in his hand. Even so, I chuckled at the thought that God's best dream for a wealthy physician might be worm research. Someone should issue an arrest warrant against God for so much subversive activity.

Chapter Twenty-three

Virginity

When two or three men gather together there is always one asshole. It is an immutable law of the universe and causes me to wonder if women operate under the same? That day's asshole was Ted.

Thankfully he left, but not before regaling us with the glory of his sexual stamina the night before, and preening on about the efficaciousness of his tool. Then, mercifully, he exited. Even so, I had a sudden urge to shower.

It is one thing to tell old tales if doing so will not reveal or injure the people involved, such oral history is one way men transfer gender data from one generation to the next. But treating the supreme act of human intimacy as a public blood sport is sickening.

Wilson acted quickly to shift the mood.

"'Debbie Do-it' we called her." Wilson hooted, shook his head and slapped his knee.

"She knew what she was doing but I didn't have a goddamn clue. She took me by the hand, I mean literally, she really did. It was my friend Eddy's fifteenth birthday and his mom was throwing him a party. I was where I always was at a party, in the kitchen eatin'. Eddy's mom made ribs like they used to, you know, where it just falls off the bone. Mmm mmm. Anyway, Debbie sashays through the door wearing this little blue dress. A little blue dress. Man, I still remember that dress. It was cobalt blue, flimsy thin and ended about an inch below her crotch. She kinda wiggled her hips when she came through the door. Who teaches them to do that anyway? So she smiles, wiggles her hips as she walks into the kitchen and, without ever slowing down or skipping a beat, she takes my hand – the one that doesn't have hold of a rib – and leads me out the back door. Leads me out the back door."

Wilson's face turned serious. He grimaced as if to suggest he struggled to get every detail exactly right.

"It's raining and I'm like, 'Hey, it's raining.' But Debbie's smiling big and acting girlish. She leads me down the back steps and into the night that is just as dark as her shiny skin. We go into a little old shed Eddy's grandpa used for getting away from the women. There was a raggedy old chair in there and a workshop. But it was dark. I mean it was *dark*. But no matter, Debbie pushes me down in that big chair and sits across my lap. She takes my hand and moves it real slow up her thigh. My heart was racing and those ribs were trying to crawl back up my throat to see what all the action was."

With that we burst into laughter, followed by catcalls and 'Amens'.

"Now she slips her fingers outta my fingers and pushes my hand around that soft inner thigh and right onto the softest, loveliest thing I ever did feel. You got to realize," he said, looking around the steam room at each of us, "up to this moment I only kissed a girl once, but here I am with my hand on her pussy. So I just sit there with my hand between her legs. She starts moving that thing up and down, real subtle like, just a little up and down. All I do is hold it in my hand like I'm cupping my balls, 'cause I don't know I'm suppose to be putting my fingers inside or anything. She moans and pushes my hand, trying to show me what to do without saying anything other than those little bitty moans. Then she starts moving her hips up and down a little more hoping I'll get the hint, but I'm too stupid to know that I'm supposed to be doing something. I just sit there holding her twat and kissing her lips."

Every one of us was shaking his head up and down, silently testifying to the recognition of that terrible moment when a girl is waiting for a boy to do what he doesn't know how to do, because shared ignorance among young boys was so heavy on bravado and slim on details. In the days before Internet porn, where every detail of male fantasy is graphically spewed onto the screen, specific information on the performance of sexual acts was woefully incomplete if not thoroughly inaccurate.

"Finally Debbie pulls away from my mouth and yells down at me, 'Put your finger inside goddamn it, and move it up and down! And move it up and down!'"

We exploded with laugher.

"Shit!" Hamm yelled as he jumped up.

Wilson had fallen into a slump next to Hamm and lay there motionless.

"Shit!" Hamm yells again. "Fuckin' shit!"

Kokomo pushed open the door and was gone before I even realized what had happened.

The torso of Wilson's body slipped down off the bench, falling against Hamm. When Hamm jumped up gravity brought Wilson down to the floor with a nauseating thud. I froze. Some invisible force pushed me violently into the corner and all I could do was watch as Hamm fell to his knees, placed his mouth on Wilson's and sent air into his lungs. Hamm pushed on Wilson's chest in a jerky up and down motion, alternating between breath and motion.

Hamm thumped then blew, thumped then blew, thumped then looked over his shoulder at me with fierceness gleaming from green eyes. His look shouted louder than any voice could and released me.

I took one step to cross the steam room and knelt beside Wilson, taking over the mouth-to-mouth as Hamm administered the pump, pump, pump motion. Kokomo violently swung open the door, pulled a bench from the shower room in front of it to keep it open, and pushed me aside. He had a battery-powered defibrillator and when Hamm saw it, he backed away. In the chaos and horror I was suddenly aware of faces peering through the door. "Shlap. Shlap." Wilson's back arched upward. Kokomo put his ear to Wilson's chest. He took a pulse. "Shlap. Shlap." Again Wilson's body separated from the bleach white tiles.

Suddenly the faces in the doorway behind Koko disappeared and figures in uniform pushed through. EMTs barked orders and someone pushed me out of the steam room.

It was all slow motion from there.

As if warriors in the aftermath of battle, Kokomo and Hamm separated themselves from the murmuring gaggle of observers. Hamm leaned face-first against the shower wall, head buried in his arms to hold in the scream.

Koko, his massive chest and thigh-thick biceps powerless to make a difference, leaned limp with his back against the wall next to Hamm. His eyes were shut but his lips opened and closed, rapidly mouthing silent prayers.

I crossed the threshold away from the area altogether and plopped down on the nearest bench. Sitting there I hovered outside myself watching everything. My hands were in a white-knuckled clasp over the top of my head as if I was reinforcing my skull against internal combustion.

Squawks from Walkie Talkies and the voices speaking into them, all still inside the steam room, rained and echoed around the silent faces of the waiting.

"Shlap. Shlap." Again and again followed by silence.

A minute or an hour passed, I don't know, but I saw the EMTs lift Wilson onto the cart and cover him with a sheet. Hamm heaved gasps. Frodo and Estefan sat ramrod straight next to one another on a bench like birds on a wire. Kokomo was still leaning against the wall with eyes closed. I felt warm tears washing my cheeks, tasted the salt, felt the wail being pulled up on a fishhook from inside my stomach, heard it shatter the air.

"Wait," Kokomo whispered loudly to the EMTs. They stopped, one on each end of the cart and another with bulky boxes of equipment in both hands. "Men!" Kokomo's voice cracked in the strain to be audible. He cleared his throat. "Men," he said louder the second time. "Gather 'round Wilson."

Zombies, we shuffled toward the mountain beneath the sheet. We surrounded Wilson as the EMTs stood their ground, cattails around a pond.

Kokomo began to pray and whoever was next to me slipped his hand into mine. I slipped mine into the man on the other side who, it turned out was Hamm. Koko somehow enclosed us in a bubble and we were suspended for the moment in nothingness – no grief, no horror, no thought. His words were at one and the same time predictable, astounding, and utterly eloquent. For a moment we were held, all of us, in Kokomo's strong arms.

Then the bubble popped, the EMT's ordered us away and Wilson disappeared.

No one knew what to do.

We were standing there frozen to our spots until Hamm walked toward the door. I followed him. Others followed me. We climbed the steep marble steps with weights on our ankles. At the landing I looked up from my shoes for the first time and at the top of the steps, peering down on our pitiful silent procession was Maggie, Gina and Rebecca. At the top of the steps I fell into Gina and Rebecca with relief, bodily aware of the difference between the power of men holding hands and the comfort of repose in the arms of women.

At the ping of the elevator everyone turned to look down the hall. Speechless we watched the EMTs exit the building with Wilson. Haltingly at first, the silence gave way to questions and the endless re-looping of the story began. Repetition is a numbing agent that escorts survivors through grief and helps to hone horror into pithy descriptions easily repeated over and over. Numbness is grief's analgesic, almost palliative.

Epilogue

The Heart Will Go On

I will never forget the image of Hamm slipping to his knees and taking Wilson's big head into his cupped hands and placing his own mouth over Wilson's. It contrasts so sharply from Hamm's scowling exit the first time Wilson poured eucalyptus elixir onto the steam pipes. The distance we have all traveled across presumption, projection and prejudice in the steam room is held in the memory of Hamm's effort to save Wilson and the heaving tears that poured out the seams of his powerlessness afterward.

We went to Wilson's funeral and met his wife and children for the first time. I think his wife was surprised by the presence of so many of us from the 'other side' of Main Street. We were a study in contrast; guys like Roger and Estefan amidst hip hop musicians and culture.

Afterward, I went with Hamm, Estefan, Frodo and Kokomo down to the waterfront along Buffalo's harbor where we leaned over the rails and smoked cigars. We smoked them for Wilson as we watched gulls and cormorants glide and dive into the water. Kokomo didn't smoke because he couldn't bring himself to soil the temple of his body, but he kept us laughing while we sucked on cheap stogies in Wilson's honor.

I miss him.

Weeks have gone by and the steam room has been empty except for one lonely occupant. Roger has been singing sad songs all alone in the steam room as if to purge the sacred chamber of its angel of death. The rest of us have walked by, heard Roger singing, paused and unconsciously lowered our heads before walking to the showers.

Before Wilson died, Roger's voice evoked a puzzled or even repulsed shaking of the head rather than a reverential lowering of the chin. In the days following Wilson's sudden expiration, Roger was a kind of sentinel holding a lonely vigil that was a balm of healing for the rest of us. It's an odd quirk of human nature that takes one and the same person, or even the same idea or behavior that under normal circumstances is obnoxious, and suddenly transforms it, if even for only a moment, into a kind of blessed medium.

Roger sang and sang his musical soliloquies with a special mournfulness. Bette Midler's "The Rose" and Led Zeplin's "Stairway to Heaven" complete with air guitar solo. But the most haunting was "The Heart Will Go On," that title song from the *Titanic* soundtrack. It has been goofy Roger, the silhouette of his body sitting cross-legged and traceable through the fogged glass and steam, belting out Celine Dion's lyrics with a resonant charm that brings mist to the eyes of anyone who knew Wilson.

It took weeks before I could put my hand on the door handle and open the steam room door again. When I finally poked my face through the crack, no one was in it and the clear air and florescent light made the tile gleam sweaty and dirty.

The part of me that now sees this chamber as an empty tomb hesitated, wanting to recoil. But at the same time, another part of me that was missing the sacred juju of the steam room was placing a foot through the door.

I heard myself say a wee prayer even while picking up the ratty old green hose and spraying the thermostat. I turned to spray off the part of the bench where Wilson had been sitting and the floor onto which he fell then realized I was being idiotic.

The familiarity of the rumbling and rattling pipes cooed to me like a bedtime lullaby. I leaned against the wall, stretched weary legs out along the bench, and closed my eyes.

I was home.

In only seconds Hamm entered. I looked up without saying anything. We nodded to one another the way men do. He sat down and sprawled.

Something was different about Hamm.

Through the haze of steam I looked at a man whose features seemed more lined and defined than I remembered, even noble somehow. It was Hamm, I think to myself, but he looked different.

I wanted to shake the thought from my head but I didn't.

The difference was surely just my perception rather than in any change that had taken place to mark him physically. Sitting there before me was the man who instinctively fell to his knees, placed his mouth over Wilson's, and valiantly tried to share his own breath of life with another. He was the man who would not give up trying to save Wilson and only, hesitantly, stepped away when the EMTs ordered him to. Hamm was not different all of a sudden but I saw him with new eyes. Fitted with the lens of that horrendous experience, I saw traces of elegance and nobility that were invisible to me before.

It is humbling to be reminded that there are whole constellations in the field around us at any given moment, that are invisible to our limited vision until experience or grace suddenly fits us with an improved lens.

Hamm stood up quietly. I could see he had something in his hand. I squinted to make out what it was but couldn't see until he stepped across the steam room toward the box of cedar slats that covered the pipes.

Suddenly I knew without what it was and

then Hamm poured the contents of a tiny bottle onto the slats. Immediately eucalyptus vapors pierced my nostrils and made my bare shoulders and arms tingle as it penetrated the pores of my body. Hamm choked and coughed, sputtered and covered his mouth and then began to laugh.

He willed himself to stay.

Instead of fleeing, he laughed at himself until tears squeezed out the corners of his eyes. I joined the laughter and realized I was witnessing Hamm's memorial to Wilson. He could just barely tolerate the eucalyptus treatment but he stayed and endured his own tribute to the fallen.

·   ·   ·

In ancient times, the Bible tells us, the landscape was dotted with shrines to local gods. Whenever a shepherd had a theophany with a resident spirit or angel, he would mark the spot with a little pile of rocks. This is where the notion of an "altar" comes from – the designation of a place where God has been. Fixed altars as we have them today, or fixed sanctuaries, take this ancient idea and supersize it as if to say, not only was God here once but also God *lives* here all the time!

The Hebrew Scriptures are littered with "naming" incidents, or the explanation of how a particular place that might be in the middle of nowhere came to be called by a certain name. The place name almost always refers to some encounter with a god or an agent of God.

For example, there is a story in Genesis about when the patriarch Jacob wrestled all night with an agent of God on the banks of the Jabbok river[4] and at the end of the story Jacob named the place "Peni'el" which, the text says, means "the face of God." There are hundreds of these little references to places where an anonymous ancient traveler had an encounter with God and lived to tell about it. In response they piled up rocks or built a slightly more elaborate altar so that other sojourners and pedestrians along the way could stop and bask in the afterglow, or even have an encounter themselves.

They did not have massive stone buildings or elegant auditoriums in the ancient world, and they did not have elaborate worship exercises to attend in order to think and talk about God. Instead, they had *encounters* with God. Just as they were closer to the earth than us, because they lived with fewer barriers between their own bodies and the heat, cold, textures, odors and tastes of life, so the veil between them and the holy must have been thinner and sheerer too.

Of course they ascribed supernatural dimensions to the crowded world of elements and events we can measure today as natural and scientifically ordered phenomena, but

[4] Genesis 32:22ff

they could also perceive elements in the field around them that are invisible to us. Invisible that is, until we encounter holiness in our midst.

A sacred place is any place where God has been encountered.

Before Wilson died the steam room was sacred, marked by the stories told and the mysteries pondered there. But the day I returned for the first time after Wilson's exit from the land of the living, I was determined to mark the steam room as a sacred place. I knew that if I gathered a little pile of rocks and placed them as an altar in front of the steam room that sooner or later, probably later, the janitorial staff would remove them.

So what to do?

I left Hamm choking and sputtering all alone in the steam room and went to my locker to retrieve the Swiss army knife I carry. When I returned, without a word to Hamm, I crouched down in front of the cedar slats that cover the pipes. I carved *W i l s o n* into the wood. The next day when I returned *S t e w a r t* was carved into another plank. The next day two more names.

This went on with names carved into the cedar and then little items left on top of them – a rabbit's foot, a cat-eye marble, a keychain, an infant's little white shoe. Over time the cedar slats became a busy altar to the god of that place, silent testaments to encounters with the holy that took place inside the strange white tiled chamber.

The COE Center staff taped up warning signs about what would happen if we were caught vandalizing the steam room, and they removed the little mementos only to have other ones appear.

Some people would call this behavior religious and wonder about the rationality of people who do such things, but I don't call the ordinary presence of God religious.

Religious is what you are when you don't encounter God and you want to: chasing the muse and never quite touching it. The more you want it, the more you chase it. The more you chase it the more elaborate and intricate the God-catcher you create, until finally the landscape is spotted with huge cathedrals purporting to house the God being chased and elegant sanctuaries that serve as museums to past chases.

•   •   •

Seventeen hundred new members have joined the Robert Cohen Fitness Center since the renovation was completed. The court where I played my last game of basketball ever, having given it up in deference to feeble knees and a deteriorating back, is now a massive workout room with row upon row of the latest aerobic machines.

In addition to the fancy sliding contraption that offers me the sensation of running again, there are bicycles with monitors upon which you can chase electronic images of other cyclists through any kind of terrain you prefer: mountains, deserts, rocky coasts and even college campuses. My personal favorite is the recombinant bike replete with a video game for chasing and killing dragons while you ride.

There are sixty motion machines for climbing stairs, running, walking, rowing and biking, and each one has its own television monitor. You can watch your favorite TV show or live sporting event, bring a movie on your tablet and watch it, or plug in your Mp3 and listen to your own music while it charges. You never have to talk to another sweaty soul while exercising ever again and probably won't because of all the electronic interference.

Weight lifters need not feel excluded because there are three massive flat screen televisions adorning the wall above the free-weights and weight machine section, which occupies the other half of the former basketball court. Spinning classes have their own room, and so does yoga and Pilates. There is even a room for stretching that sports its own huge television on the wall along with a cushy mat and stretching cage.

The locker rooms have been upgraded too. New two-toned tile with complimentary colored lockers make the men's locker room of old unrecognizable. Everything is new, beautiful, enhanced and thoroughly up to date.

One thing is missing.

There was a sense of community that disappeared, dissipated like steam into the open air. A sense of community is a fragile thing, difficult to create by intention and easily lost by accident.

Dweedle comes even earlier now and leaves before I arrive. Hamm has changed his time to late afternoon. I have not seen Frodo or Estefan since The COE reopened. Rumor has it that a handful of twenty-something bankers gave Roger such a hard time he doesn't come around anymore either.

The addition of seventeen hundred new members had the effect of a dam-break swelling a river and forever changing the contours of its bottom and banks, shifting populations of fish and birds along the way. New communities within the larger one will evolve and life will go on, but in the meantime the old has been displaced.

The steam room survived.

It is no longer white, the old tile having been replaced by larger earth tone tiles with maroon trim. It is quite nice and I promised Gina we would risk another rendezvous so she could see it. We haven't seen Rebecca for months.

They tried to fix the thermostat during the renovation by placing a fancy timer on the outside of the door. It took three days for it to break down and we were back to using the hose again. My count is up to six on the number of times they have tried to make that thing work the way it is supposed to, and each time it fails. Only a week or so goes by before the old tried and true method becomes efficacious again. Now a translucent and more rubbery hose has replaced the old shredded green one. When all is said and done, spraying the thermostat works fine.

Wilson's memory, both his death and the verve and laughter in his life, still echo in the steam room. But what made the steam room sacred were the stories told there, the sorrow and hope and anguish planted by them.

Ironically, with all the new members, I find myself alone in the steam room more often than not. Steam room stories may continue being told among other people at other times but since the renovation they have ceased altogether during my moments there. But God is capricious and so I will wait.

In the meantime, the stillness of steam room solitude offers up its own sweet fruit. Sometimes sitting there, in silence, my own life stories rising up with the steam, I am surprised to see and hear the presence of the holy where I had not recognized it before. Such is the bloom of the sacred where its nectar is sipped.

 Cameron Miller has been writing professionally for decades as a preacher, pastor, retreat and conference leader, and an adjunct professor of religion. Recently he traded that work to dance full time along the imaginative border between fiction, poetry and spiritual reflection. In addition to his published poems and *The Steam Room Diaries*, he is the preacher behind the curtain at subversivepreacher.org writing articles and essays on spirituality and contemporary culture, as well as publishing weekly sermons.

You can find out more about Cameron and links to his writing at:

http://cameronmiller.org